A LOVER'S WORTH

SPAWN OF DARKNESS

S. A. PARKER

CONTENTS

NOTE FROM THE AUTHOR

First and foremost, Dell is a sex slave. Some of the situations that occur in the Spawn of Darkness Series are brutal, but integral to her character development and the story arc. The circumstances she finds herself in are confronting and not for the faint of heart.

This is book three in the four-part Spawn of Darkness series and cannot be read as a standalone. It features a strong, albeit mentally shattered female lead, and four protective High Fae Gods who will do everything in their power to protect her.

It is a slow burn reverse harem romance with sensitive and taboo subjects, offensive language, sex slavery, explicit sexual content, graphic torture scenes and violence. It contains content which some readers will find triggering and is intended for a mature audience aged eighteen years and over.

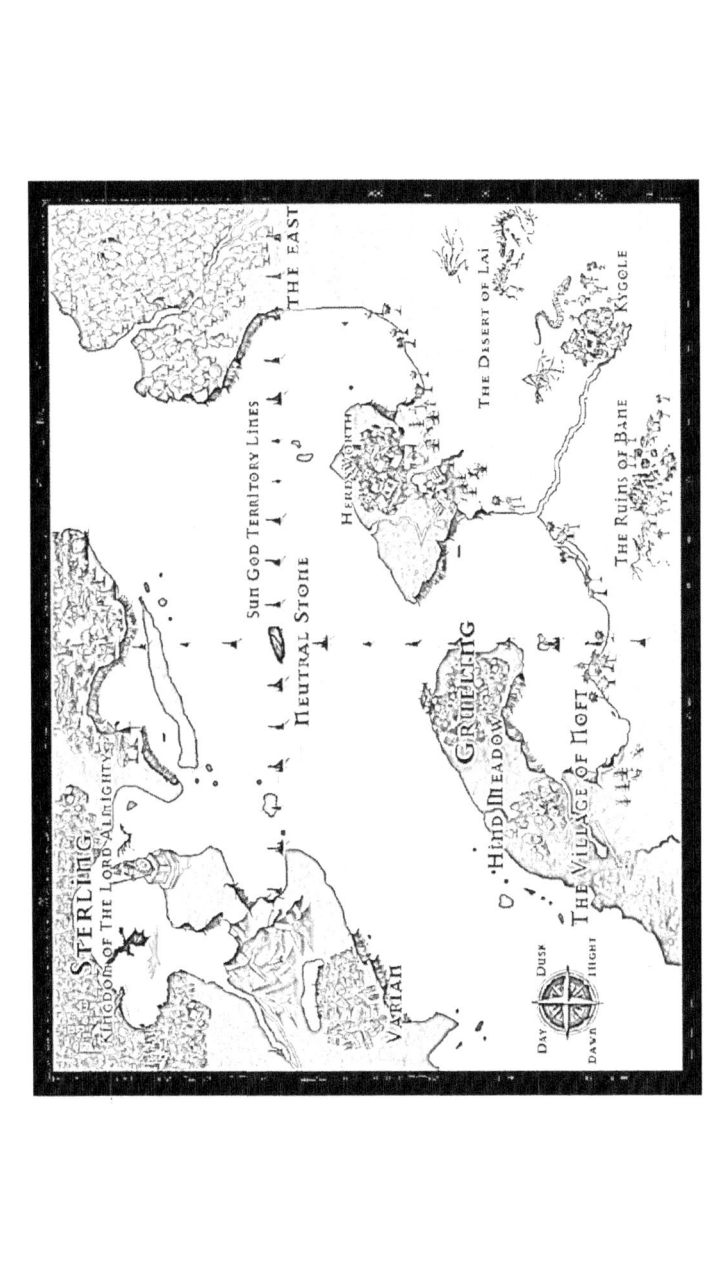

For Mum and Nana.
Thank you for showing me the true value of a woman's worth.

CHAPTER ONE

The ocean laps at my toes, sending shivers scuttling up my legs, spine, shoulder blades, through my wings then all the way to their tips. They lift, tossing themselves about in a frenzied jitter, sending sand and water raining about me.

My gaze narrows, watching the droplets fall to the ground in slow motion. They splatter, the sound like a faint beat of a distant drum, my ears flicking with the pitter-patter that my Lesser Fae hearing would never have picked up on.

I draw a deep whiff of air, the distinct tang of brine potent, tickling my overly sensitive nostrils.

Drake clears his throat, bringing my attention back to the four pairs of feet half smothered in sand, the tiny grains like a natural kaleidoscope of nature born particles.

I peek up at my Sun Gods through the mesh of salty, unruly hair smothering my face, noting their expressions have gone from shocked to positively outraged … their scents churning into something sharp and robust—the smell of anger, much more discernible now that my supreme senses have been restored.

"The white feather was yours?" Sol asks, in a voice laced with a feral undertone.

The one from my box …

No point hiding it now, it's pretty bloody obvious.

I nod, pulling myself into a crouching position, marvelling at the feel of sand dragging along my excessively sensitive skin, my wings draped like a blanket behind me.

"Fucking hell …" Kal scrubs at his face, shaking his head, as if he doesn't believe what he's seeing. "And that bottle of shit that almost knocked us out? That was from the bog we just threw you in, wasn't it?"

"I don't want to talk about that right now," I chide, doing my best to cover my lady bits.

Seems likely though, they both smell like arse. A label on the vial would have been nice. I certainly wouldn't have been against smearing the goo on my tender vagina after a hard day of fuckery, despite the foul smell.

"You don't want to talk about this right now?" Kal barks, gaze narrowing, making my hackles rise.

"No, I don't." Mainly because I'm not ready to give answers … and I'm pretty sure I can no longer lie.

"No, Dell, you can't lie," Aero snaps.

One of the downsides of being High Fae. Fuck it.

Aero's looking at me like I just broke some sort of peace treaty.

"Are you angry at me?"

His face twitches, eyes losing their molten hue, pupils expanding. "I think I need some space right now." He takes a step back, muscles clenching, hands raised. But then he's suddenly suspended mid-step.

I look accusingly at Sol who's about fifteen shades of fucked off—face red, fists clenched, nostrils flared as he takes in my wings blanketing the sand.

Yikes.

"What do you have to say for yourself?" Sol scolds in a booming voice. I'm not sure why he's so pissed off, we've got all of eternity to sweep shit under the rug now that I've got my immortality-giving wings back.

Looking over my shoulder, I gesture towards the wings splayed hopelessly behind me. "What, these old things?"

Damn. They're *really* fucking white ... how the hell am I going to wing my way out of this one?

Exhaling a dramatic sigh, I return my attention to the angry ring of Sun Gods. "Look. If we could just, like ... pretend they don't exist for a while? That would be really great."

"Are you fucking kidding?" they all bellow at once.

Tough crowd. My wings bounce out of the sand and curl around me, creating a tight little Dell cocoon. I look down at them, frowning. "I think you scared them ..."

Drake takes a step forward, his penis looking really excited to see my wings—like it's trying to reach out and touch my pretty white feathers all on its own. It almost makes up for his expression, which tells a different story entirely. "Dell, you need to be very fucking honest with us right now, okay?"

I shake my head, because I can't lie. Fuck it. "No can do, sorry."

Fuck you, Honesty Wings.

Drake frowns, jamming his fists into the pockets of his bog splattered pants.

Call me stubborn—but screw it. *They* dragged my dying body to the bog. *They* threw me in the fucking ocean. Just because *they* want answers, doesn't mean I'm ready to give them fucking answers. They should know better than to push me. After everything, they should damn well *trust* me.

"Don't make me do this," Aero pleads, and that piques my interest. I flash a look at my Dawn God and confirm, he's watching Sol with wide eyes, pupils dilated. What the hell is *he* scared of? He's the God of Dawn! He's not the one with massive, white motherfucking wings that he can't tug in and are likely going to gain some seriously unwanted attention.

But he's watching Sol ... who's watching me, studying my wing cocoon.

"I have to. We don't know if we can trust her."

Okay, my senses are tingling. I pull myself to a standing position, which happens in an explosive torrent, because I'm all swift and immortal now.

I'm poised, preparing to throw myself into that ocean—which is a terrible idea now that I really think about it. I have wings to consider, and I've just proven I'm no graceful swan.

"Drake, I need you to hold her." Sol's voice has a gravel undertone and his gaze darts between me, standing here like a feathery sausage, and Dusk. "It's taking most of my current will to hold Aero in place, and I don't want her hurting herself. I doubt she realises how easy it is to damage her wings."

He's really fucking wrong there.

I uncurl my wings dramatically, almost knocking out my Night God in the process. I can sense this situation is about to evolve into something I don't want to be a part of. Ever.

I make it about three swift steps towards the shack, where I figure I'll be able to find something to use as a weapon against these bastards, when I realise Drake isn't following me. I look over my shoulder to see him standing next to Kal, who's rubbing the side of his head from the assault of my errant wing.

Drake's arms are crossed and he's shaking his head at Sol. "Do your own dirty work, fucker. I'd rather fish the information out of her with the promise of orgasms."

I fist pump the air. Drake might just earn back his rights

of entry to my pert little flower pot. He certainly deserves a gold vagina star for that.

I hurtle towards the shack, but my glory is short lived when I'm blinded momentarily by a flash of white and Sol's standing in front of me, holding out a billowing white sheet, probably from the bed inside the shack. That asshole is fast.

He looks like he has a score to settle, and unfortunately not between my legs.

My wings spontaneously rustle about, fluffing themselves up and getting their pretty on. *What the actual fuck?* These things have a mind of their own!

Sol's gaze widens as he observes their erratic behaviour. He raises a brow, before shaking his head and grabbing me by the shoulders.

I hiss, even though my wings are still doing their little fluff dance. "Let me the fuck go, Sol!" I jerk against his grip but gain no purchase.

He spins me so I'm facing the others, stepping over my wings while awkwardly wrapping me in the sheet. I appreciate the small act of kindness to protect my modesty, even if I'm tempted to throw my leg backwards and hook the fucker in the balls.

"Stop fighting me." Sol ties the blanket into a clunky knot at my breasts, tugging firmly then double knotting it. His hands skim my peaked nipples in the process, which are almost unbearably sensitive now, sending a jolt of warmth straight between my legs. The air about us fills with the sweet scent of my arousal, and all around me, nostrils flare.

A little bit of distractive group sex with my pissed off Sun Gods wouldn't go astray right now. I throw them a hopeful wink. "How about you drop this, and we all get naked? You can even take turns spanking me if you like …"

Yeah, okay. I'm fucking desperate.

It's not my proudest moment.

Sol's arms tighten. I sink into his muscular frame, lower back pressed against ...

Holy Day God!

"Don't fucking tempt me," he whispers, lips skimming my ear. "Right now, I would not be gentle. You're not ready for that. Yet."

Fucking gulp.

"Keep still, I'm going to pull your wings in and I don't want to hurt you." He runs his fingers along the upper curve of my right wing.

Goddamn, that feels *incredible*.

I groan, sagging against him, my wings yielding beneath his touch. Fucking traitors. I've been parted from them for nineteen years and they're relinquishing themselves to Sol without my permission? Who do they think they are? I hope they get along well with my vagina, because they're on a direct path straight to the sin bin.

"That's my girl ..." Delicately, he folds them behind me, pressing them against my back. He's being so fucking gentle about it, letting his hands slowly trail over some of the more sensitive spots that literally make my eyes roll into the back of my head. I press further into his chest, trying to resist the urge to grind my aching love nest against his engorged manhood ...

"I wish I wasn't so mad at you right now." He almost sounds sorry.

There's only one reason why Sol would be speaking that way—it means he has something truly hideous planned.

That sobers me right the hell up.

"What are you doing, Sol?"

He wraps his arms all the way around me, tightening his hold and trapping my wings against my body, rendering me useless.

My pulse quickens. Sweat beading on my forehead, I jerk against his hold.

"I'm sorry in advance."

Shit.

Growling, Aero uncurls from his statue stance, moving slowly, stoically, as if he's fighting against his body's desires. He paces towards me, eyes as black as my soul.

No …

I kick out, trying to break free. Sol lifts me off the ground, so I'm hanging like a feathery little doll. I writhe and twist but it's useless, the man behind me is too strong. He's built for war, I'm built for the whore house. Big fucking difference.

"Don't do this! Please!"

Kal's curled over himself—hands wrapped around his head and I can see the conflict on Drake's face. I'm not against prying my way between a crack when I see it. "Drake, please …"

His face twitches, but that's about it. That's when I realise, he's not moving … at all.

Sol and his overpowered fucking compulsion!

"I'm not a spy!" The shrill voice doesn't sound like my own.

"I hope not, but I can't risk it. I need to know for myself."

Where's my beast when I need her?

"Some things are unforgivable, Sol! This is one of them!"

His arms tighten further. "You've left me no choice."

"Forgive me …" I don't miss the way Aero's voice cracks on the last word, his hands coming to rest around my head.

I feel the full force of Aero's power crash into my subconscious.

Motherfucker.

CHAPTER TWO

My eyes roll, mind bucking against the searing vice clamped around my conscience—like a gnarled hand clawing through my memories in a messy, frenzied attempt to sieve through the most hidden parts of me … prying at doors that have long been shut.

I bellow at the invasion, scream at it, do everything in my power to keep those doors closed.

It's no use.

One by one, the doors fly open while I scramble to keep up, fumbling over myself in my desperate plea.

The force enters, stabbing at my conscience, then retreats —like a blade being tugged from a wound, moving to the next while I stagger after it, screaming for it to look no further. For the pain to stop.

It reaches a trapdoor that's hidden in a corner; shaded in cobwebs and shadow, the handle dusty from lack of use.

I stumble forward, gasping, the scent of fear tainting my senses. "No … no, not that one, please!" I fling myself across it, sprawled, blocking the way as the door begins to rattle …

A LOVER'S WORTH

I groan, claws embedding themselves into the fleshy meat of my mind.

"Enough! I'm hurting her!" Aero's voice slices through my conscience, attempts to soothe the agony, and fails.

"Is this the memory she pushed you out of when she was at the Dawn Kingdom? We're not stopping until we have the rest." Sol's command is firm, final.

Damning.

"Fucking hell! Yes, it's the same fucking memory!"

The force thickens, the pain becoming unbearable ...

No ...

"Sol ..." I sob, spreading myself further across the trapdoor, trying to placate the rattle. "Please stop, please! I'm begging you. Please don't do this to me ..." My voice is weak, decaying.

I'm hauled out of the way, pushed to the side, the trapdoor lugged open, releasing a bright shaft of light.

I recoil at the scene now settling before me, a place I once knew—small, simple, bright ...

Home.

There's a woman, her back to me, with a giggling pile of blanket and limbs nestled in her arms.

She tosses it onto the bed.

"No ... Sol, please!"

It's useless.

I'm flung into my four-year-old body, tumbling out of the blanket, my laughter mingling with that of my mother's—warm and melodic, trickling out of us in waves.

There's the sound of fabric ripping, my tiny white wings pushing through the freshly mended seams holding the back of my dress together, doing their little happy dance.

They always used to do that. I was never able to control them.

Mum's laughter fades and her expression becomes serious. She drops onto the bed next to me. "Adeline, honey, you need to keep them in."

I look over my shoulder at the puffs of white stretching themselves wide, enjoying their newfound freedom. "It's hard, Mummy. I can't stop them. And I like having them out … it feels so good."

She sits me up and holds my shoulders, hooking my attention. The scent of her uneasiness fills my nostrils. "It's not safe, darling. Your wings won't keep you safe, not until you're much older."

"Because my Daddy's a bad man?" I ask, cocking my head to the side and fiddling with the hem of my simple linen dress. It's covered in flour, and still holds the smell of the scones we baked for breakfast.

Mum nods. "A very bad man. Adeline, you can't trust anyone but me, do you understand?"

I frown at her, pouting. "You never let me see other people. All we do is swim in the lake at night and do home things. You never take me to town with you to get supplies …"

She curls her elegant but mottled fingers around the loose tendrils of my hair, sweeping them into the palm of her hand and tugging them into a ponytail, which she secures with my favourite white ribbon. "You don't want to go to town, Adeline. Even I'm not immune to some of the stuff that goes on there these days."

I now know she was referring to her charred skin. Four-year old me had no idea, basking in my protective bubble of innocence.

I peer up at her. "What do you mean, Mummy?"

She shakes her head, petting one of my wings with gentle, loving hands. "Never mind, Little Dove. Now—do me a favour and pull your gorgeous wings in, yeah?"

I scrunch my face and ball my hands into tight little fists, imagining them as two thick ropes hanging from my back, picturing myself tugging them into my body, as Mum often instructs. But it's useless, I've got no idea what I'm doing. It's usually just dumb luck if I manage to get them back in. Sometimes it takes days. Other times, weeks.

Never minutes.

Frowning, I slap my hands on my knees. "They're stuck."

"They're not stuck, sweetheart."

"They are," I declare, folding my arms across my chest. "I think they're broken."

My mother frowns and my ears twitch, taking in a distant crackling sound. "What's that noise?" The smell of burning wood assaults my senses.

Mum's off the bed in an instant, standing by the window, peering out at the neighbouring houses in the small village with her good eye. "Oh … no." Her voice is little more than a whisper. The room blooms with the scent of her fear— distinct and sour.

"What's wrong?" I ask, shuffling forward on the bed and curling my legs beneath me so I can prop myself up in an effort to peer outside.

Mum swings around, watching me, though I can see her attention's split.

"Can you get them in?" She gestures towards my wings dancing about in fluttering motions.

I stretch them wide and scoop at the air. "They like being out, Mummy."

"Just … try, Little Dove."

"Okay …" I do, eyes closed, fists clenched. "Please, please, please go back in, little wings …"

It's useless. They don't want to hide, they want to be free.

I shake my head, causing my curly ponytail to tumble about in a whitewash of naivety. "They don't work properly."

Mum's throat bobs. I hear her heart skip a beat, can scent the anxiety seeping from her pores.

"Mummy? What's wrong?"

"Can you feel a well of warmth inside you, honey?"

I reply as I always do to this question. "No."

Her eye darts back and forth between my face and my wayward wings. I see the anguish in her expression.

I also see the moment her heart breaks.

She spins, dodging the small wooden table that holds a plate of half-finished, fluffy scones, smeared in the butter she brought home yesterday as a special treat. The butter smells salty and rich and I breathe it in, mouth tingling in anticipation of finishing our feast.

Smelling it now, reliving the moment, I realise it wasn't the butter I was smelling … it was my mother's tears.

Mummy clatters about in the kitchen, quickly filling a small brown bag with hurried movements. "Come with me, Little Dove."

I slip off the bed backwards, stretching my toes into sharp points so they connect with the cold floor, before shifting my weight and dropping myself down. I patter after my mother, my movements light and swift, following her through the door that leads to the back room we use for storing fruit from our trees in large barrels.

"Close the door behind you," she whispers over her shoulder, then jerks the trapdoor in the floor open.

I curl my hand around the brass knob and tug the door towards me, wincing at the way it squeaks and groans then clunks shut. Turning, pulling my wings tightly against my back, following Mummy down the open trapdoor, I see the storage room door has slipped the latch and is jarred open—daylight from the front room shafting through the gap.

It's not the first time that door has failed to do its job properly.

It won't be the last.

Mummy reaches past me—the rough, distorted skin on her forearm brushing against my cheek as she tugs the trapdoor closed with a soft thud.

I follow her down the dimly lit ladder—the wooden rungs rough against my hands—to where it smells like the earth, the air thick with mildew. Dust tickles my nose and I sneeze, almost smacking my head against the wood.

Mummy's hands curl around my waist and she lifts me from the ladder, tugging me into her tight embrace. My wings curl around us both as my nose itches with the scent of her fear, mixed with the smell of baked goods still infused in her shift.

"Why are you scared, Mummy?"

She presses her face into my hair and draws a deep breath. "Do you know how much I love you, Adeline?"

Tilting my head back, I beam a wide, toothy smile at her. "More than the sun." My words are threaded with conviction.

Mummy loves the sun, but I know she loves me more.

She tells me it all the time.

She nods, running her fingertips over my cheek, brow, then down my nose, tracing the arc of my face. "More than the sun, baby girl. And do you know how much that is?"

I nod, giggling when her fingers tickle the skin just below my ear. "The biggest amount ever?"

"The biggest amount ever," she repeats, rocking me gently, placing a featherlight kiss on the tip of my nose. She strides across the room filled with fluttering golden light emanating from a small lantern, drawing long, frightening shadows across the dirt walls that are littered with rocks and rebellious tree roots.

She stops before a table, crushing me against her body, pressing warm kisses to my forehead, just as she does before she puts me to bed for nap time. But it's not time for a nap yet…

"Am I going to sleep?"

She nods, inhaling a shuddering breath, features curling into strained happiness. "Yes, Little Dove. Just a small sleep."

"But I'm not tired, and it's cold down here," I say, pouting.

She shakes her head, face twisting. She presses her hand to her mouth and drags a shuddering gasp. "I know, baby. But I'll take the cold away."

I have a brief moment to wonder why her emotions are now distorting her features, her voice, and trickling from her face, before she's laying me on a long wooden table. She kisses me, smearing tears across my cheek.

"What's wrong?" I press my little palm to her cheek. She captures it with her own, holding it there, tracing my face with her eyes. "Mummy?"

She clears her throat, kisses my palm then sets it in my lap. "Nothing, Little Dove." She wipes the pool of moisture from the underside of her chin, offering me a tight smile. "You're going to have your nap now, but first I need you to roll over for me. Can you do that?" The smile tugs at the melted tissue around her mouth, though it doesn't reach her remaining eye.

Nodding, I shift my wings and roll over, sucking a breath through my teeth as my face presses against the cool grain. I shuffle, trying to get comfortable—my wings fluffing themselves up then settling against my back, trying to do the same. "The table's cold …"

Hurriedly, she smooths a wayward curl from my face, rolling the pad of her thumb over my ear, tucking the tendril out of the way. "I know darling, but you won't be able to feel it soon."

"Why?" I ask, frowning.

She uncorks a small jar, pouring green liquid onto a deep metal spoon. "Do you trust me, baby?"

"Yes."

Using her spare hand to tilt my head upwards, she offers me the spoon and I open my mouth, swallowing back the bittersweet substance that coats my tongue in an oily sheen, making me gag.

There's screaming in the distance … it frightens me. I want to ask Mummy about it, but now there's another sound nearby—the clanging of metal against metal. I'm dimly aware that it's my mother making the sound …

No.

I don't want to go here … I can't fucking do this.

I try to steer the image away. Gritting my teeth, a thick pulse throbs through my head.

Something wet dribbles from my nose. I wipe at it, frowning when I see the red smear on the back of my hand.

This never happened …

Catching movement in my peripheral, I notice Aero standing in the corner of the room. He's watching me … watching my mother … watching my memory. His skin is sallow and bland despite the delicate, golden glow fluttering about the space.

His throat bobs.

My vision wavers, blurring at the edges.

Aero's fists tighten into balls. "I'm here …"

Yeah, no shit.

The neighbour's dog is barking, it's tone frantic. There's a sudden yelp and then silence.

"How do you feel, sweetie?" My Mummy's voice claims to be calm and composed, though I smell the lie it's laced with. I was too young to understand then.

I understand now.

I understand perfectly.

"Everything feels heavy." I try to lift my arm and fail. I do the same with my wings, but they lie laden and limp. Scenting the air, I smell her rising panic—too disoriented to ponder why as she cuts away at my dress frantically, the fabric falling to the ground in uneven shreds.

Shivering against the cold, my teeth collide against each other in a delicate, steady chatter.

"Do you … do you feel tired?" Her words are baited … desperate.

I shake my head, watching Aero. "No."

He swallows, pushing a long, shuddering breath through tight lips and dropping into a low crouch, elbows perched on his knees, hands splayed across the lower half of his face.

There's another scream in the distance, the sound of wood splintering.

My mother uses a naughty word, fingers caressing my wings with cautious, tender strokes. I can feel her eyes on my face … studying me. Waiting …

A second passes.

Two.

Three.

Swearing again, she kneels, retrieves a scrap of my dress, and scrunches it into a ball. "I'm so sorry, baby, I can't wait any longer. Please forgive me ..." Her quivering hand stuffs the material between my lips, into my mouth. Something cold and sharp is pressed against my wing, right where it feeds from my back.

Curious, my wings try to lift from their place tucked against my body.

The object moves, a small, hesitant nudge as Mummy lets out a strangled sob. I feel a sharp sting, then the heavy pressure of my mother's body over mine, not quite an embrace.

The sting grows into a roaring, agonising explosion of

pain that makes my body jolt and quiver, hips rising, legs seeking purchase against the smooth table top.

I scream, terrified and confused, but my cries are muffled by the material in my mouth; muted by the fog suffocating my senses.

"I'm sorry baby … I'm so sorry." The words, stained in sorrow, leak from her mouth between heaving strokes of agony.

Through the pain, the fear, and the realisation of what my Mummy is doing to me, is the sickening sound of a saw drudging through bone and cartilage—a noise that has haunted my dreams ever since.

Grind.

Grind.

Grind.

She's taking my wings.

She promised me she'd never hurt me, she told me she loves me more than the sun … but Mummy is taking my wings.

I glimpse a blade in my side vision, its teeth smeared with a thick, pink substance and dappled with tiny, sodden feathers stained ruby red. Finding some strength, my wings stretch out in a pathetic, heartbreaking attempt to flee the agony—arching unnaturally as they curl and squirm against the searing pain … against my mother.

Weakening, I continue to fight in a pitiful attempt to flee from the horror.

It's useless.

I can't escape my mother's shuddering weight trapping my small, writhing form.

Aero approaches through the haze of pain, holds my limp hand in his own, more phantom blood dribbling from my nose.

"I'm here." His breath catches, grip tightening. "Stay with me, baby."

It's lost on me.

He doesn't realise yet, but I'm already gone.

The first wing falls, thudding onto the soil, white feathers stained in red. Warm liquid pools across my back, dribbling down the sides of my body, collecting on the table beneath me.

"You're being so brave. Halfway … there, sweetie." Her words are serrated with shuddering breaths.

Bile fills my throat, presses against the material in my mouth, making me gag. My remaining wing is tucked tightly along my back—as if she thinks it will do her any good.

My mother shakes her head fiercely, features bunched, canines bared. The blade is pressed against the juncture between my back and wing, metal teeth sinking into the sensitive flesh.

My fingers curl, nails biting into Aero's hand and drawing phantom blood, though he doesn't flinch.

Grind.

Grind.

Grind.

That wing, too, falls to the ground.

My mother's weight lifts, though I'm too broken to move.

Everything is so silent.

Everything smells bland.

Everything feels so much more … *simple.*

They are the vaguest of thoughts as my mind scrambles for its senses, fumbling over pain and the absence of my wings. I don't feel like I've just lost a couple of limbs … I feel like I've lost an integral part of my *soul.*

"Fucking hell." Aero's grip on my hand tightens, shaking, tears tracking down his cheeks. He watches my mother intently as she pours a foul-smelling substance over my back, rubbing it on all the tender spots. I'm too broken, too busy choking on this newfound reality to struggle.

I'm past the point of fighting Aero for purchase on this memory, I'm past the point of anything. After all I've been through, all I've lived through, it's reliving this memory that's finally breaking me.

She gathers my ponytail and tucks it to the side, then grabs a nearby lamp with an unsteady hand. Aero brings his lips to my palm, pressing them against the damp flesh.

I hear a sound, like a cork popping and then a terrible heat engulfs my back, searing the places my skin has been mutilated.

I'm aware that I'm screaming, though there is no sound. I try to move, but I'm paralysed. There's no escape from the agony, the smell of burning flesh, the terror.

She lets the fire run, patting me in places to contain the blaze, slowing it to melt my flesh just the right amount.

I know now she was hiding my scars with new ones … then, however, I thought she was burning me alive.

I thought I was dying.

Part of me even hoped that I was. Though I didn't understand what it meant to die, I knew it meant everything stopped.

At the time, that sounded just perfect to me.

Finally, the terrible heat subsides.

"All done, sweetie." Her voice is fractured, so too my thoughts, as the fog that had settled over my body begins to lift …

She washes herself down with water from a bucket, movements hurried, hands shaking. She slices her wrist, smearing her blood over my body, masking the scent of my agony with that of her own.

"Go to sleep, baby. When you wake, go searching for a

woman, not a man. Take your things with you, do you understand?" Her words are hurried. Clipped.

A tear slips from my eye, cutting a direct path to the wooden table to mingle with my blood.

She reaches down and strokes my cheek, her remaining eye wide and unblinking. I flinch but lack the energy to push her hand away, though I watch her face twist in torment when she sees me recoil.

She dips her head and kisses me on the forehead with quaking lips. "I love you, Little Dove. Be strong ..." her words are stained in moral pain. I feel the warm press of her tears on my face, her hand fisting through my hair. She moves away and, without even a backward glance, takes the rungs two at a time and climbs out the trapdoor.

For years it troubled me that she didn't look back.

I think it still does.

There's a heavy thump overhead, the sound of something being dragged across the floorboards. I pull the sodden material out of my mouth and drop it on the ground. Stifling a whimper, I haul my legs beneath me, teeth grinding against the tug and pull of raw skin across my back.

I flop from the table, landing in a heap of crumpled limbs. Uncurling tentatively, I stand, covered from head to toe in my mother's blood ... in my own.

I take small, jagged steps towards the ladder, past my discarded wings with blood leaching from their stumps, towards the sound of harsh voices and tossed furniture. A growl reverberates through our home, through my body ... followed by a shrill yell in my mother's voice.

Somebody's here. Something's not right.

The trapdoor is heavy. It takes all of my four-year-old strength to push it open enough for me to squirm through. When I do, I see that the door leading into the front room has been left open enough to allow a thin shaft of light into the storage room. On my tummy, the wood chilling my bare body, I edge forward until I'm as close as I dare to the open door. I tilt my head and peek through the gap.

My hand flies to my mouth, stifling my gasp as I take in the scene—the shattered coffee table, shards of wood cast around the room in explosive disarray; the scones now buttery clumps littering the ground, stained red from the blood smeared across the floor.

But more terrible than anything else is the sight of my mother, lying in a crumpled, bloody heap.

A man stands over her, wide and solid, platinum hair striking against black eyes peering out from beneath a thick hood. Vivid, white wings are splayed behind him, smothering the small space of our living room. "It's like you have nine fucking lives," he snarls.

Mum responds in a weak, gurgling groan and the man huffs his displeasure, lip curling in a poisonous sneer. "You're fucking weak, Mare. Unworthy." He dips, gripping her by the arm and hauling her against him, allowing her blood to smear across the sterling chest-plate shielding his vital organs. "You're going to die knowing just how weak you are. Knowing a woman's worth is *nothing* compared to a man's."

I try not to cry out—Mummy told me my father had white wings. She told me he was a bad man.

"Just … fucking … do it, Edom." Her voice is spiked with desperation.

I thought she was done with life. I thought she was giving up. Now, replaying this memory, I understand the true value of her actions.

She was protecting me.

He reaches down, thick fingers curling around the hilt protruding from a sheath slung at his hip, and pulls a long, silver blade from its confines.

I gulp back the lump that has risen in my throat. The

agony of my wounds, the searing pain of my burns, it all fades away ... replaced by a deep ache in my heart.

I know what comes next.

Something shifts behind me. I barely notice when I'm lifted into the air, my limbs suddenly losing their rigidity. I'm tugged into the warmth of a body, snuggled close. Aero's hand wraps around the back of my head, tilting my face into his neck. He presses his other hand over the side of my face, covering my eyes, his chin coming down to rest amongst my tangle of hair.

Though I don't see it, I feel the moment my father slices through my mother's jugular with that silver blade—Aero's body jolting as his arms tighten around me.

I didn't cry when it actually happened. I was too afraid.

I cry now. Great, heaving waves which ravage my body, shattering me into shards too complex to piece back together again.

Aero makes soothing noises, running his hand through my hair.

I'm too far gone.

I always have been.

White wings are wasted on me, so is the power they undoubtedly come with now that I've matured—because deep down I'm still this small, broken child who had my wings sawn off by my mother, then watched my father kill her in cold blood.

"Enough," Aero whispers into my hair ... then he's yelling. *"Enough, God-fucking-damnit!"*

My knees buckle, though I'm vaguely aware of Sol holding me up and Aero's hands dropping away. Sol releases me and I land in a heap on the sand, the sickening thud of fists colliding with flesh almost loud enough to drown out my screams.

I can't stop.

My hair is smoothed from my face. "It's okay, Dell. It's okay …" Kal's voice is plagued with uncertainty.

"Take it away!" I beg.

The agony continues, devouring me from the inside out as darkness pulses within me. Blood dribbles from my nose.

My beast cracks an eye open. I can sense her prowling to the surface. I don't have the energy to hold her back.

"Please! Kal! *Please* …" My shrill yelling tears at my throat. I taste blood, red spittle flying from my mouth, landing on my hands which I barely recognise as my own anymore.

No more scars.

I have no more fucking scars.

I scream again, raw and guttural.

"I'm going to take the pain away, baby. I'm going to take it all away …"

I become silent, like … fucking instantly, blinking up at Kal whose face is twisted with concern.

"Golly, I was so sad!" I smile, pushing tangled hair from my face, and sit up, all perky and shit.

Kal's looking at me like I'm a broken vagina, a cute little crease over his brow. I reach forward and finger it. "I like this, *so* adorable." Wow, my voice is really merry, even if it is a little raw from all that unnecessary screaming.

Aero is pinning Sol to the ground. They're covered in blood and hissing at each other, like all the anger in the world belongs to them, and them alone. I wonder why Sol isn't compelling Aero? Strange.

"Make love, not war!" I chime, though they totally ignore me. I shrug. "I always thought Sol and Drake would be the ones to kill each other, never imagined it would be the two sadists to have it out. Guess it makes sense now that I stop to think about it ..."

Kal tugs the makeshift sheet dress over my boob, which had broken free for a peep at her spunky Sun Gods. Cheeky wench. The sheet's no longer pristine white, and I try to frown. It's so hard to get blood out of white sheets ...

"Where's Drake? I owe him a gold vagina star." I giggle at that and Kal arches a perfectly manicured brow.

I can't wait to slap that happy vagina star all over Drake's body.

"Actually ..." I smile at Kal. "You didn't hold me down either! Gold vagina star for you too! Where do you want it? Anywhere?"

I don't realise I'm shuffling forward until Kal pins me in place by my shoulders, cursing under his breath and shaking his pretty head. "You fuckers sort yourselves out, I'm taking her to Night. Don't bother coming over until you're done killing each other."

I squeal in excitement. "Night? Can't wait! Can I have the room with the pretty candlesticks again? Although, I'd like to share a room with you ..." I pout. "Actually, you probably have your harem to attend to. That's okay, I understand. I can watch, you won't even know I'm there!"

"Fucking hell." He groans, grabs my hand, and flashes me to the Night Kingdom, landing me in a large, ornate bedroom before sauntering off to the balcony where he does his pretty glowing thing. It saps away at the last of dusk and makes me want to dance the maypole with him.

"You're so pretty when you glow!" I gush, twirling a curl around my finger and contemplating the Kal canvas I want to lick all over. The glow fades from his skin, but he's still looking fucking delectable as he turns and strolls towards me. "Night really suits you!"

He rubs at his temple, that little crease between his eyes

still prevalent, stopping almost close enough for me to rub my nipples all over him. I arch my back, managing to skim them across his chest, and smile.

He frowns, taking a step backwards, though I don't miss the bulge growing in his tight, leather pants. I press my hand to my face and stifle a giggle.

"How are you feeling?" There's genuine concern in his voice, no idea why though.

"Like a million tokens! I'm just so happy, the world is a great place!"

"Mhm." He crunches his eyes shut, squeezing the bridge of his nose with his thumb and forefinger, and takes a few heavy breaths, looking very fucking dramatic if you ask me.

"You should smile … you look so beautiful when you smile. It highlights that little chin dimple." I reach forward and try to mould his face, but it just won't seem to co-operate. "Hmm … seems that dimple doesn't want to come out to play today. Do you want me to show you how it's done?"

He doesn't answer, so I give him my biggest smile ever. "Shee?" I say through exposed teeth, pointing at my pearly whites. "Ish weally eashy!"

He shakes his head, rubbing his hands over his face and scrubbing at his frown.

Was worth a shot.

I shrug, stepping past him and walking to the balcony. It's got a railing and would be a great place to sleep. Although I have wings now … hmm. Not that I could ever use them before. I doubt I'd have much luck now, even if I were falling to my death after rolling off a balcony mid nap.

I look over my shoulder at said wings—they're really fucking beautiful; bathed in the light emanating from his excessive lair that's all shiny black stone, mottled with silver threads and softened with black velvet accents.

"Hey, Kal! How pretty are my wings?" I'm pointing at

them with a great big smile plastered on my face, just in case he's not sure what I'm talking about.

He clears his throat and walks towards me with a small smile that looks forced. I'm not angry about it though, because there's no room for anger with all this happiness swirling around inside me.

He leans against the door frame, folding his arms over his chest, making his biceps pop deliciously. "They are ... the most beautiful wings I've ever seen."

Well, fuck me. My vagina drooled at the same time my wings did a little happy dance, fluffing themselves up and now looking even better.

I see the moment his smile turns genuine as he observes my little wing dance. I also see the moment that gaze turns hungry. I take three steps towards him before he puts out a hand, signalling for me to halt, his smile disintegrating.

"Don't, Little Dove. I need to calm my thoughts." He closes his eyes and breathes deeply.

I'm not sure why he would want to repress all the happiness my vagina has to offer, and my wings are super pumped for the idea, too. They're literally fanning themselves out so far that it's difficult for me to turn around on this balcony, which now seems really fucking small.

From my peripheral, I see the city below lighting up with Fae orbs and large, illuminated spires as the night begins to swallow us whole. I pout, trying to work out how I'm going to turn around so I can take a long look at that pretty view behind me, while I mull over the fact that he just called me 'Little Dove.' Such a sweet coincidence. My mum used to call me the same. That makes me so unbelievably *happy*.

"My wings are broken ..."

Kal opens an eye at that, then he actually fucking groans, looking like he's starved of something. Probably my pretty wings. I wish he'd preen them for me, they're practically screaming for the attention, stretched to full wingspan and all.

"Can you pull them in?"

I like the way his voice sounds, like he's on the verge of pumping me full of his cock juice.

I shake my head. "Nope, they like you too much. I think they want to see yours. Yeah, that's a good idea. They can rub up against each other." I nod enthusiastically at my great plan. All I need now is a willing Night God and we're good to go!

He puts his face in his hands and breathes deeply. "Sun give me strength ..."

I suddenly feel really fucking sleepy, and even my wings are drooping when I tilt back into Kal's arms and fall fast-the-fuck-asleep.

CHAPTER THREE

I wake in a massive, black, screw-twenty-people-at-once bed, alone, laying on my belly so I don't crush my gorgeous wings. They do a little dance for me, appreciating my gratitude, and I smile widely, arching my back.

My wings fan themselves wide, stretching all the tiny muscles and sending shivers of ecstasy along my spine. "Damn, that feels good." They stretch again, at a different angle before settling into a neat, tight little parcel of pretty.

I note I'm no longer wearing my blood-stained sheet. Instead, I'm wearing a cute, black dress with a low back for my wings to sit over. Kal for the fashion win!

The object of my thoughts strides in from the balcony, with a chin full of prickly shadow and heavy eyes ringed with the hint of red. Poor man, he doesn't look like he slept at all, though I can't find it in myself to feel sad about it. I throw him my biggest smile ever because someone needs a dose of all my happy.

He rubs his face and yawns. Actually, I don't think he's even noticed I'm awake…

"Long night?"

Jumping, he looks at me like he's surprised I'm in his God quarters, then sighs with another one of those cute little frowns. "The longest. Did you sleep well?"

He sits on the bed next to me, which is about ten feet away because the bed's so fucking large. "So good! Best sleep ever. And I've woken up feeling so happy I could burst. How great is *that*?"

He averts his gaze. "Really great."

I try to catch his eye, unsuccessfully. "What's wrong?"

He shakes his head. "I don't want to talk about it."

I frown, but it's forced and totally feigned, because I'm thrilled as fuck. "Do you feel guilty about making me happy? Because you shouldn't. I feel *amazing*! Never better."

He studies me for a good few seconds, broad shoulders hanging heavily, before he finally answers. "I love seeing you smile, Dell. I just wish it was genuine."

"It *is* genuine! Look how happy I am!" I point at my smiling face. "You need to lighten up, eternity is a long time to be sad."

He lets out a deep huff of emotion. "I agree, it is."

I feel like he meant more by that comment than what I'm actually absorbing. Anyways.

"Where are the others?"

He shrugs, laying back against a big, fluffy pillow. "Alive, they've all checked in a few times. Sol, a lot more than that."

Wow! I feel like that should make me mad, but instead I'm just so damn happy about it! I love my Sun Gods, every single one of them. "Great, I can't wait to see them all later." My wings do a little puff dance before settling themselves back in again. I motion towards them. "I think they're excited, too. Maybe you can all pet them at once? They could do with a good stroke from my four Sun Gods, they're practically screaming for attention."

He grumbles low in his chest, closing his eyes and shaking his head. "No, Kal. No …"

"No, what?"

He shakes his head again, but I can see the bulge growing in his pants. I lift a brow. So does my vagina.

Ooooh yes.

My wings push themselves wide, running a few white feathers over his luscious lips. His chest rumbles and his eyes snap open, glancing first at my wings then sidelong at me, the midnight blue swiftly fading to black. "Dell …"

My wing tugs back then rubs herself over him again. "Yes, Kal?"

We lay there watching each other, ten feet apart though it feels like we're so much closer than that right now.

He draws a deep breath. "I can't control myself with you and I don't want it to seem as though I'm taking advantage of your fragile state—I don't want you to see me that way when I remove the happy web."

I hear him, I really do. I know what he's saying, but I just don't care. "Kal—you *helped* me. You showed me kindness when I needed it the most, and now I'm so happy! I just want to show you how much that means to me …"

He groans, twisting to face me. "That sounds really, *really* tempting, and I *know* I'm going to regret this choice … but I can't. I want you to be emotionally sober when I have you for the first time, Little Dove." He strokes my wing and I shutter the urge to moan, because she fucking loves his Night God fingers running through her feathers.

And he said *'first time.'* That means he intends to have me *more* than once. My vagina does a little twirl then drops it like it's hot, because she's fucking ecstatic to hear the news.

"I want to show you that you mean much more to me than an impulsive fuck. I want to put you on a pedestal and *worship* you. I want to make your body feel so good that you never think about the fucking East again."

I lift an eyebrow, but he just shrugs.

"We talk. Not going to apologise for that. Just know that after I'm done with you, after I've shown you everything I have to offer, the thought of selling fruit or anything else mundane is going to be so fucking outrageous."

"It's good for a woman to have a backup plan, though."

He shrugs. "Yes, but we're not letting you out of our sight. We've got you now, and I, for one, am not letting go."

Wow, my heart just exploded. Usually I'd duck my head at conversations like this, but *that* just made me really damn happy. I shed a joyful tear and beam the biggest smile *ever* at him.

He runs his fingers over a particularly tender feather, and I groan like an animal as my eyes roll into the back of my head. "That feels amazing!"

There's a bright flash and I feel the bed shift, then the press of his knees along the sides of my body. He leans down and whispers in my ear in his velvet 'fuck me' voice. "Just your wings, Little Dove. I think I know what they need."

Yeah, no shit. They need his God hands all over them. "Don't be afraid to slip yourself inside—my vagina needs a little attention too. Just saying. She won't object, neither will I."

He chuckles and shakes his head. He probably thinks I was joking.

"Not this time, Little Dove. Just your wings … they're *so* fucking beautiful."

They rustle their feathers, giving him a good glimpse of just how beautiful they are.

He runs his finger along the upper edge of my left wing, sending me headlong into a quivering spasm. Holy fucking Night God, that's the sweet spot! "Do it again … please!"

He does, really … fucking … slowly.

I groan, tilting my hips, hoping he'll absentmindedly slip the head of his penis into my raging well of warmth. My vagina's cheering me on, she's so pumped we're finally on the same team.

"You like that, don't you?"

I grab a couple of fists full of coverlet. "Don't … stop … ever …"

"Oh baby, I've only just begun."

Yes. *Fuck yes.*

He runs his other hand along the upper edge of my right wing at the same time, and my body curls in on itself from all the Night God pleasure he's dishing me.

He does the same again, but with more pressure applied, and I almost spontaneously combust.

"Fucking hell. Your scent … your body wants me so fucking badly."

I nod, tilting my hips further, showing him *exactly* where my body wants his cock.

He laughs, the sound deep and throaty, making me want to smear my vagina all over him, though he gently pushes my hips back down to the bed. "Nice try. You're not ready for my dick."

"I fucking am!" I plead.

He works those magic hands over my wings again, paying attention to the area where they spawn from my back, kneading his thumb into a particularly sensitive part.

I combust, wings going taut as my entire body spasms in pleasure, screaming loud enough to wake the whole neighbourhood with my rowdy orgasm that goes on forever. I swear to Gods; at one point I'm worried I'm going to spend the rest of my life in orgasmic splendour. It wouldn't be so bad, but it also wouldn't be very productive.

Finally, the orgasm fades to a gentle warmth and my

wings seem to wilt, my body relaxing. Kal curls around me and tenderly kisses the side of my face …

Hang on a minute … "Where are my wings?"

Gone! *Poof.* Just like that.

I look at Kal, whose eyes are *jacked*. "You're telling me, all I needed was a *wing orgasm* to pull the bastards in?" I sound pissed but I'm actually so fucking excited. All I need to do is pop my wings out at the wrong time, and one of my Gods will stroke the ladies until I squirt vagina juices everywhere to get them back in.

He nods. "Seems that way …"

"Fuck yes."

He laughs through his nose, somehow managing to make it sound sexy. "I could tell they were hankering for it—it's unusual for them to be so demanding, or sensitive. I doubt they would have responded so well for someone you don't care about though …"

The statement sounds more like a question to me.

I nod. "Probably right. Can I rub your wings too?" I just want us to rub each other's wings all day, every day, for the rest of our immortal lives.

"No, Dell, not today. Not while you're under my net, anyway." He pushes a strand of hair behind my ear—the movement so delicate, I smile. "Like I said, I wouldn't be able to stop myself. It would be like bedding a drunk woman, and not knowing if she was *actually* into it or not. I'd never do that, so I won't have you now." He draws a deep breath. "Despite how much I fucking want to."

I roll my eyes, pushing myself onto my back. My vagina's pouting, even though she's still quivering. Giving him a sideways look, I note his firm cock pressed against the seam of his trousers. "Then I guess you're spending the day with your harem?"

He taps his finger to his lips, watching me, his gaze quizzical. "No."

"No?"

"No. Despite Sol's jesting, I barely ever go in there. I certainly won't be going in there anymore; I have your gorgeous fucking wings to keep me on my toes."

I roll onto my stomach because I feel them popping out of my back at the mention of their gloriousness. He's right ... they *are* fucking gorgeous. They do a little fluff dance, so I reach back and pat them with the tips of my fingers.

"What do you mean ... you don't like your harem anymore?"

He quirks a brow. "Do you really want to talk about this?"

"Yes, I need you to spell it out for me."

"Well, this is their haven ..." he says, cautiously. "A place they can enjoy each other and be safe from the King." He pauses, clearing his throat before continuing. "As long as you're okay with it, they will have a home here for as long as they wish; despite the fact that I no longer have sex with the few who are partially interested in my dick."

Hang on a minute ... "Do you mean ...?"

"Most of them are only interested in other women? Absolutely."

Huh.

When I walked through that room the first time, I did notice most of them were too preoccupied with each other to even notice our presence ...

And here I was, thinking Kal was the biggest man whore of the bunch. Instead, he's liberating his very large group of vaginas ... just not with his God rod.

I wonder if this man has any other carefully veiled secrets.

He quirks a crooked smile. "Like I said—I intend to put you on a pedestal, Little Dove."

Smiling, I stroke that really eager erection, but he grabs me firmly around the wrist, halting my progress. "Don't."

I roll my eyes for probably the tenth time today, but retract my hand and go back to fondling my feathers. "Did you have sex with that girl, the one at Kroe's establishment?" I ask, in my happiest voice ever.

He rolls onto his back, sucks in a deep breath then slowly lets it out. "I did, and my dick was so soft, but I had to have sex with her because you fucking *wished* me too." His voice has a resentful undertone, which I ignore. "Anyway, I ended up doing other things to get her off, seeing as it felt wrong being inside her. Didn't take much to get the poor thing to orgasm, she was so starved of pleasure."

The story makes me feel really fucking happy, and I nod enthusiastically. He clears his throat, eyeing my wing that's brushing his brow, having decided it's a good time to seek some more attention from her Night God.

Greedy things.

"I like that you're so happy about that story, it actually means you're really pissed off about it. And it's a big fucking turn on knowing you're feeling possessive of me …" He turns his head to the side, looking me in the eye and paralysing me with happiness.

I smile so damn widely. "Can you blame me? They should rename you the God of Sexy, and Wing Orgasms." I think on that for a moment. "God of Wingasms, let's go with that. The 'sexy' part speaks for itself. Loudly."

He smiles, flashing those gleaming canines that I may or may not picture being embedded in my neck. "I also like how the happy web tears down those highly fortified walls of yours."

I nod. "I have no walls. Just happiness. Speaking of tearing down highly fortified objects …" I gesture to his throbbing erection. "Want a hand with that?"

He groans, rolling away from me and only just missing another caress from my over enthusiastic wing. He settles on his back, knuckle poised between his teeth. "Just ... give me a second."

That thing looks like it's going to need more than a second to deflate, not that I'm an expert or anything. Actually, I am. I'm practically a professional penis deflater. Never looked at it that way ... it puts a nice slant on the whole 'whore' thing. "So, what are we doing today?"

He waves his hand in the air dismissively, eyes screwed shut. "I can't talk to you right now, even your voice is making him ache."

Aww, he's speaking about his penis as if it has its own identity. I think I'm rubbing off on the bastard. "Whoops, no talking then."

He levels me with a glare. "Dell ..."

I'm running my fingers over my lips—pretending to button them together—when a tall, dark, sexy hunk of man meat saunters into the room. When he sees me, he stops mid-step, mouth wide open, eyeing my wings.

Kal sits up swiftly, groaning in the process—probably because the action gave the excited party goer between his legs a bit of friction. "Cassian ..."

Cassian's solidly built—muscled arms and chest tapering to a thin waist. His black hair is longer than Kal's, tickling at a three-day old shadow, a roguish fringe dangling in eyes which are ... purple? Odd. The tip of a tattoo is visible, peeking up by his shirt collar. I'm curious as to what it is.

Cassian's gaze drops to Kal's erection and he clears his throat, turns around, and slips his hands into his pockets.

"Wait here, Dell." Kal rolls off the bed and I swear to Gods, my wings pout. "Do not fucking move, do you understand me?"

I beam a smile at him. "Sure. No problem, glorious God of Wingasms."

Cassian clears his throat and Kal winces, striding towards Cassian with shoulders that look like they need a good massage. He leads him through the open doorway and closes the doors behind them.

Private conversation, it seems.

I smile, because I don't mind being left out *at all.* In fact, it only makes me *happier.* But twiddling my thumbs gets boring after about thirty seconds, and my face starts to ache from smiling too much, which only makes me smile *wider.*

Thinking about my sexy Night God's orgasm giving hands, I pull my left wing forward, giving her a little inspection, and decide she could benefit from a tidy up. She fluffs herself up at that thought, probably because she's all enthusiastic about looking her very *best* for all four of her Sun Gods. Especially Kal. He gave her some serious attention, and she seems pretty excited about showing him her appreciation of his wise hands.

I'm mid-preen when Kal storms back into the room with Cassian in tow, both looking stern as shit. I tilt my head, observing them walking side by side …

Hmm, they walk the same.

"Dell, we're go—" Kal stops abruptly, cocking a brow as the determination in his gaze melts, replaced with something akin to … curiosity? Shock? "Are you … *preening?*"

I look down at my pretty feathers, then back up at Kal. "Yeah … do you like it?" I stretch my freshly fluffed wing out wide, a proud smile plastered across my face as I eagerly await his approval.

Cassian blushes … strange.

"Turn around, Cassian, and leave the fucking room."

Ohh, assertive Kal. My vagina sniffs the air.

"Yes … Sire." Cassian turns and leaves the room, a barely repressed smile nudging the corners of his lips.

Kal takes a step forward, then pauses. "Baby, are you preening them for me?"

I nod enthusiastically and the smell of male arousal thickens in the large space we're occupying.

Cassian chuckles in the hallway. I don't know what's so funny, but I appreciate that someone's finally meeting me on my happy scale.

Kal takes another step forward, hands out in front of him, as if he's approaching a rabid animal. "I love that you're preening your feathers for me, Little Dove, but let's just keep it for my eyes only, okay?"

I pout, though it's a super smiley pout, and drop my hands from my pretty feathers that are practically gleaming now. "What if I want to preen them for Aero, Drake, or Sol?" I know I'm a bit greedy, but I think all my Sun Gods deserve to see my feathers in tip top shape.

"That's okay—just not in front of strangers. Okay?"

"Meaning Cassian's a stranger, and not welcome in my harem of hotties?"

Kal winces, and Cassian makes a choking sound.

"No. Cassian is out of fucking bounds. No preening in front of Cassian. Ever."

"Got it." I consider for a moment, frowning. This is all very strange. I just wanted to make my wings sparkle for my Night God. "But … why? What if I want to preen while I'm walking down the street one day? The need just … you know, pops up?"

Kal takes a few quick steps forward, suddenly standing in front of me. He pulls my hand away from my wing—which I was absentmindedly preening again. Wow, I'm efficient. Multi-tasking like a fucking boss.

"Let me put it into perspective …"

I can tell he's trying really hard not to look at my pretty wings, and my chest swells with pride. My preening skills must be *fantastic.*

"Preening is a sign you want to mate with someone … in other words, it's foreplay. It would be more acceptable for you to lie down on the street with your legs apart stroking yourself in front of a crowd than it would be for you to preen those glorious wings of yours in public."

Oh.

Right.

Well then.

Told you I need a fucking manual. That explains the scent of arousal …

Kal cocks a brow, probably because all the blood just drained from my face, though my smile is wider than *ever.*

"So … no preening in public places?"

"No. Not unless you want me to drag you into a dark corner and sink my teeth into your neck."

Wow. Now I'm blushing. Head spin.

Kal laughs and tugs me up, pulling me from the bed. "I'm going to get these beautiful wings of yours to tug into your back, then Cassian, my general, is going to accompany us to the throne hall. Sound good?"

I cock a curious brow at my sexy Wingasm Master. "Sounds good to me! What's the occasion?"

"Some urgent business, but I can't leave you here or I risk dropping the happy web. But if you want me to drop it, I'm *more* than happy to dr—"

"No! Happy web stays on!" I blurt.

He frowns. "I thought you'd say that. Turn around, let me see those beautiful feathers you prepared for me."

I spin, my smile practically splitting my face in two.

Fuck yes … wingasm time!

CHAPTER FOUR

I'm trailing behind my Night God and his hot general, trying to ignore their tight buns wrapped in matching leather fuck me trousers.

The hallway of the Night palace glitters with its black stone threaded with silver striations, enhanced by the light flooding in through wide-open arched windows running along one side. It takes a sharp turn, as though following the curve of the mountain it's carved into, rather than fighting against its confines. There's a break in the windows in the form of an expansive archway which leads to a glistening balcony . . . without rails.

Pausing, I note the men are deep in conversation as they walk ahead, so I curl my hand around the arched frame and draw a deep breath of the fresh, crisp air flowing in through the space. Jasmine and verbena. Glorious.

I walk onto the balcony, creep towards the edge, and gasp in sheer fucking wonder.

Holy Kingdom of the Night.

I can't be sure, but it looks like we're perched atop a giant, hopefully dormant, volcano. A vast crater lake of sparkling turquoise lies at its centre, circled by a sprawling city arching up the internal edges, its buildings appearing to be carved from the very mountain itself. No two are the same— perhaps created by the individuals occupying them, expressing their individuality.

The Night Kingdom palace dusts the entire upper ring of the volcanic crater. There are balconies—one of which I'm standing on—jutting out sporadically below a sky caped in powder blue. The sun is sending a long shadow across one half of the bowl, leaving the other half in glistening, glorious light.

I take another step towards the threshold, the light wind tugging at my hair, and a small chunk of stone breaks away from the edge.

Oops. I hope that doesn't knock some unsuspecting High Fae the fuck out.

"Little Dove …"

I spin to see Kal behind me, hand extended, a look of concern shadowing his face.

"Don't worry, I'm not going to jump," I beam at him.

He offers a forced smile. "How about we move away from the balcony, yeah?"

"Fine." I take his hand and he leads me back inside. "I was just appreciating the pretty view. I never knew your kingdom was so beautiful!"

I love this happy web. It's like being perpetually high on life with no worries in the world!

Cassian is waiting for us ahead, leaning against the wall, watching us with barely masked curiosity.

"I had you housed on the ocean side when you were here last—just to be safe."

"Meaning you thought I might be a risk to your people … a little whore like me?" I'm skipping along beside him now, because one can only smile so much before it overflows into happy steps.

He shakes his head, halting my skipping legs by grabbing my chin. "Don't be mad …"

I practically beam at him. "I'm not!"

"Fucking happy web," he grumbles under his breath, storming ahead.

I shrug, skipping after him, feeling as light as a feather.

Kal passes Cassian. "Stick with her and remember what we discussed."

Cassian releases a deep, dramatic sigh. "Why don't you just put her to sleep? Then I can tuck her behind a column until you're done?"

I laugh at the suggestion.

"Because she will roast my fucking balls. Just do as I said."

Cassian nods then drops in behind me as I continue to skip down the hall. He's probably making sure I don't get distracted by happy thoughts and pretty views.

Kal disappears around a corner ahead and I turn to face Cassian, who's looking at me like I've gone mad, as I skip backwards along the hallway. "So, we're going to the throne hall?"

"Yes." His tone is clipped and he wiggles a finger, indicating for me to turn around again.

I oblige, but not before I've done a couple of twirls, just because.

We round the same corner Kal did, bathed in golden, morning light, and I come to an abrupt halt.

An enormous archway opens up to a space that resembles the colosseum in Grueling—the one they use for the weekly whore markets. Except this is not a whore market at all, and it's certainly a lot bigger and substantially grander than the colosseum. This one is carved from the same silver-threaded black rock as the hallway, and is big enough to house thousands of people in the stands. As it is now, those stands are at least a quarter full, wings of various colours and tones perched behind spectator's backs.

A podium juts out from the tiered seating, upon which sits a large, silver throne, glowing in the light streaming through the open archways like a not-so-distant star. Kal strides across the podium and the crowd erupts in cheers as he sits in his shiny God seat, hand raised. The roar of the chanting crowd settles into a murmuring rumble.

"Just stick with me, and we won't have any trouble," says Cassian. He's watching the ground at the base of the colosseum, as if waiting for something.

I open my mouth to ask what, but he wraps his warm, calloused hand around my wrist and drags me off along the upper, outer ring of tiered seating, which curves around the many columns reaching skyward. I'm smiling so fucking widely, because I just *love* being dragged around and told what to do.

We stop about midway around and I have a full view of my God of Night sitting over there on his glowing chair, and whatever is supposed to be happening below. Kal is wearing an impassive mask, his face all hard lines, jaw firmly set. He doesn't look like the Kal I know … he looks like a ruthless fucking God.

My vagina licks her lips and I take a step forward, intent on telling him exactly what she thinks of him right now, but Cassian hauls me back in place, onto a high bench.

"Nuh uh, you stay right here."

"But my vagina needs to speak to my Night God," I plead.

"Fucking hell …" Cassian shakes his head, grumbling under his breath, but keeps a hand firmly clenched in the back of my shift, anchoring me in place.

Kal lifts his hand and the crowd falls silent. A man is dragged through a doorway at the base of the colosseum by two grey winged men with staunch shoulders and taut expressions.

The man they are dragging has dirty blonde hair and a bloody nose. His hands are cuffed in iron—evident by the red burns around his wrists. There's a smear of dirt crossing the right side of his face, and his clothing is torn in places, though his tunic and pants look fine enough to belong to a nobleman. The wings spawning from his back are a gentle shade of pastel blue and I marvel at their beauty.

The two men release him and he falls to his knees, facing Kal from his spot on the floor. One of the guards grasps a handful of his greasy blonde hair and pulls, arching his neck and forcing him to look at the God seated above him.

What the fuck is going on?

"Victor." Kal's voice echoes throughout the vast space. "You kneel before me, convicted of two counts of torture, two counts of rape, and one count of murder. How do you plead?"

Holy.

Fucking.

Hell.

This is a trial.

I jump up and down in excitement, my smile so wide it hurts.

"It's not the time," Cassian hisses, shaking his head and tamping my overeager hands.

Kal's gaze shifts to me, a deep crease shadowing his brow.

Oops. I chew my bottom lip and sit on my splayed fingers in an effort to suppress my joy.

He drops his attention back to the man on the ground beneath him.

Even from this distance, I can make out the beads of sweat coating Victor's brow as he works his lips around silent words, blood trickling from his nose, splattering on the ground by his knees.

"Answer me!" Even I jump as Kal's booming voice tears through the air, compelling the crowd to sit straighter in their seats.

"G—guilty!" the man finally spits out, closely followed by a heaving groan as the blood continues to flow … It looks like our convicted criminal was trying a bit too hard to lie.

Kal stands and a girl, no older than sixteen with long hair the colour of wheat to match her pretty wings, is led onto the podium by a woman with a round face and warm eyes. She gives the girl a nod of reassurance and positions her next to the throne, before taking a step back. The girl's shoulders are curled forward, her face smeared in snot and tears which she wipes away with the back of her hand.

"You will be judged by the only person who has the right." Kal indicates the girl. "Your surviving victim."

The man on the ground pales, his chest heaving as this reality seems to settle upon him heavily.

"You will either be given the death penalty—committed to the same fate as your other victim; be removed of your wings and therefore your immortality, condemned to a short life with the Lesser Fae; or the third, and merciful option— cast out beyond the shrinking boundaries of the Night Kingdom with the understanding that one day, those boundaries may no longer exist, in which case, you could once again live among us."

A roar goes up from the crowd and Kal silences them with a raised hand, then turns his attention to the woman standing beside him.

She is no longer crying. Instead, a sharp sneer plagues her face …

Me? I'm jumping up and down with excitement again. I can't fucking *wait* to hear the answer!

"Shed him of his immortality," she hisses, fist pumping the air. "Cut off his wings!"

The crowd erupts in a tremulous cheer and I jump up and down, arms in the air, giddy with joy.

Kal's eyes ink over, right before my legs crumble beneath me and I curl forward, dry retching. Kal propels himself off his platform, landing in front of Victor with a thud, then slowly uncurls his body to tower over the cowering man.

"Fuck …" Cassian's voice is etched with concern. "Are you okay?"

I raise my head to see Kal produce a serrated blade. He brings it down to press against the bud of one of those beautiful, pastel blue wings.

I retch again, holding my hands over my chest, feeling like my heart is going to shatter into a million pieces.

"Dell? The happy web?"

"Gone," I groan. Fucking gone.

My wings explode from my back, surrounding me in a protective motion. I'm lifted and propelled around the edge of the colosseum, just as that familiar 'grind' begins to plague my ears.

I scream into my feathers, the sound drowned out by the excited howls of the mob below. We exit into a corridor where Cassian sets me down onto the cool, stone ground. I hear triumphant shouts, the first wing undoubtedly being tossed to the side.

"You have no idea what it's like to live without them!" My voice is a strangled shriek, my hands hauling at my chest which feels like it's been flayed. "There has to be another way …"

"This is the way things are done. Our only option that's fair."

I grind my teeth together, try to drown out the distant blood curdling howl, the nauseating drudge of blade against bone. I press my hands over my ears, rocking my body back and forth. "There has to be another way!"

"You have a better idea? One that will stem the flood of your father's wrath? Be my fucking guest!"

I flinch at the harshness of Cassian's tone, at the horror of the words and the terrible possibility of what they might mean …

I shake my head, *clawing* at my ears, crunching my eyes shut. "Just make it stop … make it fucking stop!"

"Cassian, go. I've got this."

Kal's rich tone settles heavily upon me, and I'm lifted against a hard chest stained with the scent of blood, right before I pass the fuck out.

Warm water swirls over me, trickling beneath my wings, still wrapped around me in a tight, feathery cocoon. Arms hold me, muscles rigid, smothering my small frame and consuming me. The rich tang of sulphur fills my nostrils.

I smile. Oh … sweet, sweet, happy web.

"How are you feeling?"

I open my eyes and squint at the brilliant blue stain of sky fanned overhead. We're perched against the edge of a deeply set, thermal rockpool, thick puffs of steam wafting into the air about us, making the sky look milky in places. "Fucking perfect."

Kal sighs, then rumbles beneath me. Grumpy Kal.

I push up and his arms loosen so I can unwrap myself from my wing cocoon and spin around, straddling him. A small waterfall of warm water cascades into the pool, splashing over Kal's shoulders and bare chest … no longer smeared in blood.

"You cleaned yourself off." I smile, running my hand over

his chest, lifting my gaze to meet his, seeing that my God of Night's face is taut and strained. "Oh dear … do you need me to show you how to smile again?" I mould his mouth into a tight grin, chewing on my tongue in concentration when he doesn't readily comply.

He grabs my wrists in a firm, unyielding grasp. "Stop, Dell. This has to stop."

"What?"

He shakes his head. "You can't live in this happy web forever."

I beg to differ. "Just take your wish, then use the boost to keep powering the web, and we're good to go. No need to get all grumpy faced about it."

"That's not what I mean. This isn't healthy …"

I shrug. "I feel pretty healthy. And happy."

"But it's a fucking lie." He drops my wrists, then wraps his hands around my waist, lifts me up and plonks me on the ledge before moving off to the far side of the pool, clad in nothing except tight, black briefs that snuggle that delicious arse of his.

I cock my head to the side, enjoying the view, when he leans forward and pressed his hands to the ledge, highlighting every muscle and rivet in that very well-defined back.

I slap my smiling face. Concentrate, Dell. Kal's pissed, you need to make this right.

A brisk chill sweeps over my damp skin and I push off the edge, back into the warm embrace of the water and wade towards him, wings drifting long and sensuously behind me. I look around at the cluster of beautiful pools surrounding us —a fountain of turquoise flowing against a stark white background of mineral deposits, cascading down to the azure waters of the beach far below.

Wow. Fancy. Guess that's the perk of living on a hopefully dormant volcano.

I return my attention to the brooding Night God. He's watching the horizon with, I think, feigned interest.

"I've discovered that if you have a happy web over your mind, then you forget all the bad in the world, and everything seems really fantastic. Perhaps you should try it?"

He shifts his heavy glare to me, a look that would probably send me running if I wasn't so happy right now. "And how's that working for you, Dell? How's it fucking working?"

"Perfectly! Otherwise I wouldn't have suggested it, silly." I don't know why he's bombarding me with questions he should already know the answer to.

He shakes his head and turns to grab me, hauling me against the edge of the pool and boxing me in; warm breath tickling my face. "The Dell I know wouldn't have jumped for joy when that young girl chose to have her rapists wings sawn off—she would have felt the pain as much as I did, despite the fact that he was a fucking monster."

I sigh in delight. "This conversation's making me feel so good inside."

"The Dell I know," he growls, ignoring my joyful outburst, "was the one who broke down in that hallway when I lost control of the happy web. *That's* the Dell this world needs. Not this one." He gestures to me sharply.

I throw my head back and laugh, the happiness rolling off me in delicious waves. "Don't be silly! That Dell is so broody."

Kal takes my chin in his hand and lowers my face so he can look me in the eye. "The world needs *you*. The proper you. Not this … *seemingly* perfect version."

"What are you saying? You don't like me like this?"

"I like you any which way I can get you."

I try to frown, but my face is too busy smiling. "Then ... what are you worried about?" Confusing Wingasm Master.

He shrugs, drawing a deep breath and slowly letting it out. "The Dell I *love* is beautifully broken. No matter how much we try, I doubt we will ever be able to put her back together entirely, but I wouldn't have her any other way."

Well ... fuck. That's heavy. Too bad he's filling a cup that's already brimming with happiness.

He searches my eyes, the sapphire depths bouncing back and forth across my gaze. "Dell?"

My stomach rumbles. I smile and pat it with my flattened hand. "Is it too late to request breakfast in bed?"

Kal sighs, closes his eyes and rubs at them, before plastering a super forced smile on his face, making me giggle hysterically.

"Sure, Little Dove. Let's do that."

"You going to eat that?" I point to the small pile of untouched, honey glazed bacon sitting on Kal's plate. He's barely eaten a thing.

"No, I don't think I will. Knock yourself out, Little Dove." Kal pushes back the covers and climbs from the bed. Leaving me alone with my mound of food, he walks to the balcony and peers out, muscles coiled, leaning against the doorframe.

"Are you okay? You seem tense." I pack my mouth full of bacon, chewing patiently while I wait for my Night God to grace me with an answer.

"This gift is both a blessing and a curse right now." He turns to face me. "I'm just pacifying the issue, probably making things worse for you in the long run."

I think on his statement, chewing bacon and watching him with what I hope is a sultry gaze. "Did you know," I swallow my mouthful, running the tip of my tongue over my lips, "That your meat is *utterly* delicious?"

Kal blinks at me, clears his throat and shakes his head. "I'm going to go take a cold shower. I'll be right back. Don't do anything I wouldn't do."

He stalks off, face shadowed and stern. I set my empty plate to the side, watching him pull open the giant stone door that leads through to the washroom. It must be real goddamn heavy. Probably the reason he's so jacked.

I clear the plates, stacking them neatly on the table by the door then plop back onto the bed. I spend a few minutes running my fingers through my curls, though it gets pretty boring after about thirty seconds. All this happy is so overwhelmingly exciting.

I try my hand at a wingasm, something I quickly realise is impossible. They just don't get as excited by my touch as they do Kal's.

I tumble out of bed, do a couple of twirls and skip outside, drawing a deep breath of air when I reach the edge of the balcony. I can smell *everything*—the freshly tilled soil down there by the big, black barn-looking place; the jasmine creeping up the side of the palace and even the manure they've used to fertilise the garden of that little house across the lake. Go me. I take another deep, delicious breath and lift my arms high—my wings shivering with joy behind me, dipping and curling.

I want to run, to dance, to frolic in the ocean …

I want to … *fly.*

Spreading my wings wide, I climb onto the edge of the balcony and throw myself off. I fall for about three seconds— white wings trailing hopelessly behind me—before I realise I can't work them … at all. The thought makes me *super* giddy with happiness.

I giggle, filled with the joy of falling and the knowledge that I'm probably going to die.

Something flashes in front of me and I thump against the hard chest of Kal, who wraps me in his arms.

"Well, hello there!" I call out over the sound of the rushing air as we plummet towards the ground at breakneck speed. I give him my biggest smile ever.

He's definitely not smiling back, killjoy.

"Tuck your wings in, *now!*" he bellows.

Wow, grumpy Kal.

Laughing, I do as he says, because he's looking at me like he wants to strangle me, and it's a *very* angry look. Perhaps he's lacking in the happy department because he's dishing it all to me?

He flips us over and in one glorious, surging movement his wings appear—big, black and fucking beautiful, pumping the air in strong, magnificent sweeps. I can't resist, they're so shiny and pretty and ... and ...

I reach out to touch one.

"Don't, Dell. This is a bad time to do that," he growls over the hiss of the wind.

"Booo." I giggle ... this is so much fun.

We land back on the balcony and Aero's standing there, arms crossed, wearing his glorious bronze God gear and looking like he's ready to start some mayhem.

I throw him the biggest smile ever. "Hey! I just flew ... kind of."

Aero shakes his head, sharing a look with Kal that's a little condescending, which I choose to ignore.

"Looks like you're learning the hard way how difficult it is to manage our girl, Kal."

'Our girl!' Aww. I do a little dance on the spot, because it's hard to move around when you have a Night God glued to your back.

He releases me, shifting a couple of feet to the side, looking me up and down with a frown before glancing at Aero. "I really want to tell you to go away, but I actually think I might need your help. I only left her alone for three minutes and she threw herself off the balcony in a fit of laughter. She's hard to manage when she's so jacked up on happy." He shakes his head, looking unnecessarily baffled.

I laugh. "Because I've never felt much of it before, silly!" That's just the funniest thing *ever*.

Aero looks at me like he doesn't recognise me, head cocked to the side and studying me intently, all residue of 'angry Aero' gone. He scratches his head. "Wow, yeah. I only get her internal dialogue, but when you pair it with what's *actually* coming out of her mouth …" He looks sidelong at Kal. "How have you managed?"

My wings do a little puff dance and spread themselves wide, curling around so they caress both of my currently present Sun Gods. "Ohhh yeah, come in for the wing cuddle, boys! My ladies need a good rub down after all that hard work."

Aero lifts a brow.

Kal groans, his own wings doing a little fluff dance in response—though I can see him struggling to hold them in place, tucked behind his back. They're even shaking. It only makes me smile more widely. His wings *totally* want to hug me back.

"It's really fucking hard, Dawn. *Really* fucking hard."

Aero clears his throat and shifts his belt.

I glance down at their crotches, clapping my hand over my mouth as I do so. "Yes, it is boys … yes, it fucking is."

CHAPTER FIVE

*A*pparently, I now need flying lessons. They probably saw how much of a natural I was and decided they should fuel the talent rather than suppress it.

"Aren't you worried I'll flutter off to the East? Because that really does sound fun. Not that I want to run away from my amazing life, but it would be nice to see my fellow ex-whores and dish them some of my happy."

Kal gives me a look that's about five parts confused and five parts 'she's a crazy bitch', before he sighs dramatically and tugs his top over his head, allowing me a peak of his spectacular abdominals.

Aero shakes his head as though he doesn't know what to do with me, though I have a pretty simple solution to that problem. He could bend me over his knee, spank me, then pump me full of his Dawn juice?

He growls and his eyes begin to ink over. I throw him a wink and wave hello to that pretty face of his.

Kal steps between us, blocking my line of sight to my sexy Dawn God, but allowing me a full-frontal view of Night Godliness. He looks over his shoulder at Aero. "Tune out, man! I told you! She's not fucking sane right now, okay?"

"To be fair," I chirp, "I'm not sure if I've ever had all my eggs in the nest, if you get what I'm saying. Don't want you guys to have buyer's remorse. Best you know now that you're only getting around six out of twelve tokens from me, lads."

Kal shakes his head again, looking like he just doesn't quite know what to say to that.

"She asked for this, Kal."

My Night God spins to face Aero, wings out again and taking up an unnecessary amount of room—though *my* wings seem to think otherwise, reaching forward and trying to caress them. I smile, curling my hair around my finger and enjoying the show.

"Are you saying I should leave her like this? Because if you are, I seriously question your motivation. In fact, I'd be justified in putting you to sleep for an entire fucking *century.*"

The many moods of Kal never cease to make me smile.

"That's not what I'm saying," Aero responds, his voice calm. "I'm saying you need to stop beating yourself up about it."

Kal growls but tucks his wings in tightly, much to my disappointment. He spins around and cocks a brow. "It's hard not to. I mean, look at her." He gestures towards me.

I smile-pout, bopping my head to an imaginary happy beat while toying with my hair.

Aero winces.

"Sooo … flying lessons? You two can't wait to see these pretty ladies in action again, can you?" I point to my wings, currently reaching in their general direction. The needy tarts are hankering for a good rub down.

Kal frowns. "It's better than finding you splattered on the rocks somewhere after attempting to do something you know nothing about."

I feel like that comment should offend me, but instead I jump up and down, clapping my hands, happiness spewing out of me in torrents. "Flying lessons!"

"I'm not sure how much longer I can take this … I'm chewing through my energy to keep her happy, which is only going to do more damage in the long run. It's costing me progressively more by the minute to keep her this way, which means beneath the web, she's not in a good way."

My Gods study me like they're watching some fascinating bird, a really pretty one, of course. My wings rustle at *that* thought, because they know they're fucking stunning.

"I know what you're thinking …" Aero's eyes narrow.

Kal cocks a brow. "Think it'll work?"

"It's worth a fucking try—shock her system a bit, give it a reboot. You're right, she can't live like this for the rest of her life."

"Like what?" I look from one to the other but, receiving no reply, I breathe on the shiny coffee table and draw cute little condensation hearts.

"The longer this goes on, the more painful the whiplash is going to be when you peel off the web."

"Where are the others?" Kal asks, shaking his head and frowning at me.

"The Day Kingdom, trying to sort their differences. Not going too well."

Kal nods. "What a surprise. I'm sure Sol won't mind …"

"Won't mind what?" Again, no answer, which makes me laugh hysterically.

"I'll tell Cassian I'll be heading out—good luck with that." He gestures towards me. "Try not to make her laugh too much."

Kal leaves and I turn my attention to my Dawn God standing in front of me, looking all sad and shit. "Turn that frown upside down, big man."

He sighs and drops onto the seat next to me, receiving a mild assault from my over-enthusiastic wings.

He clears his throat, ignoring the feather trying to work its way up his nostrils. "I need to talk to you."

"Ohh, okay. Serious talk. I can do serious." I attempt to school my beaming features into neutrality, with very little traction. "Damn, this isn't working, is it?"

He shakes his head.

I give up, still smiling from ear to ear. "I can guess what you're going to say. You're concerned I'm internalising all my sadness, and that I'm going to start having conversations with my hand, or something, to cope with it all … right?"

The world's smallest half smile curls the edge of his lips, but I call that a fucking win. And then it's gone again.

"I like everything that happens inside your head. It's the footprint of who you are, what you've been through … and though it's fucking heartbreaking that your mind has been forced to twist around itself to protect you, it's you." He taps his temple with a finger. "I miss you … in here."

"I'm still here." I gesture to myself in a wide, sweeping motion.

Aero shakes his head. "Baby, you're not." He tucks a rogue curl behind my ear, leaving his hand to rest at the side of my face. "And I understand that, I'll be forever haunted by the look on your face when you realised your mothe—" His voice cracks on the last word and he breaks my eye contact, shaking his head.

I stroke his big God chest. "Aww. There, there …"

He grinds his teeth as he watches my petting hand try to work some magic on his sadness. "Dell, it's time to come back. We can work through it together, but we can't do that if you're not here with me."

I laugh, loud and hearty, drowning Aero's dramatic sigh.

Kal storms back into the room, a hand pressed over his heart. "I said no fucking laughing, dick."

Aero works to uncurl my wing from his arm, unsuccessfully. "That one hurt?" he asks, frowning at the cute little feather grip my flexible as fuck wing has on him. Really, it's quite impressive.

"Yeah it fucking hurt … every time she laughs she literally rips away chunks of my energy."

My laughter kicks up to maniacal at the thought of all that energy he's pumping me full of. I'm wiping away the happy tears streaming down my face when Aero reaches his hand out for mine. "Come with me, dear …"

Aww, Aero just called me 'dear'. Kind of sounded like he was talking to a crazy old lady, which makes me laugh so hard I almost wet my panties. He sidesteps my assaulting wing coming in to claim his other arm and flashes us to the Day Kingdom.

We land in the super sparkly dining room with the fantastic view that's just as beautiful as I remember, and Kal quickly follows.

"I'll get them—they're probably in the throne room arguing over whose cock's the biggest." Kal flicks a glance my way. "Try to stop her from throwing herself off the edge again."

I laugh hysterically, curling forward and grabbing at my stomach. "That was so funny. I feel like it should make me angry, but it just makes me want to run my tongue over his arse." I look at Aero, who's watching me with a bemused expression on his face. "Do you ever get that?"

He raises a brow. "The desire to run my tongue over Kal's arse? No, can't say I do."

I shrug. "Your loss. It's a really ripe arse. Speaking of which, isn't it about time your lips became acquainted with my labia?"

Aero chokes and I pat the fucker on the back. "Looking after you lot is hard work. I'm realising more and more that I really *do* have my work cut out for me ..."

Drake, Kal and Sol flash into the room—Sol in full fucking wing span. I squeal with delight, running forward and launching myself into his arms, curling my hands around his body and snuggling him tightly.

"That's code for 'she really fucking hates you right now', in case you hadn't worked it out," Kal offers, being a super helpful Night God. He's so handy to have around.

Sol clears his throat. "I figured that one out myself, thanks. Jerk."

"I'm *so glad* to see you!" I gush, then throw the same smile at Drake, who's looking like he chewed a lemon. "And you! I owe you a gold vagina star. I'm going to put it everywhere, if you know what I mean." I throw him a wink to emphasise my point, right before I take a big whiff of Sol's neck. "Fuck me, you all smell so good! Want to watch me preen my feathers? You can all sit in a circle around me while I make the ladies gleam."

Sol looks pained, which confuses me, because the scent of arousal is thick in the air.

Yeah ... they can't *wait* to watch me run my fingers through my feathers for them.

My wings curl around to stroke at Sol's, but he tugs his back into place and peels me off by my hands, holding me infront of him like a baby honey bear.

"Someone take the girl. I don't want her sobering up and thinking I didn't give her the personal space she *actually* needs from me right now."

That makes me so happy!

"Come here babe, I've got yah." I latch onto Drake when he comes in for the snuggle.

Sol clears his throat and Kal winces.

Aero makes a sound that could be amusement. "You brought this on yourself, remember."

Sol stomps to the table to pour himself a glass of water from a sweating jug, and I snuggle further against Drake's chest. "I missed you and your magic orgasms. Though Kal gave me some just by massaging my wings—turns out all I need is an orgasm for them to tug back in again. Cool, huh?"

Growling like a savage, Drake snaps his attention to Kal, who throws his hands up in a look akin to exhaustion.

"You've no idea how hard it's been! Those wings are so fucking demanding." Kal gestures to my feathery lady friends, which are now wrapped entirely around my Drake, who clears his throat.

"Yeah, I can see that."

I smile into his neck. "They like you too. They like all *four* of you … they're a bit fucking greedy if you ask me, but I'm not complaining. I'm sure I can find a hole to accommodate each of you."

Cue a Sun God groaning symphony that makes me sigh in delight. "You guys are so cute! Screw the flying lesson, let's bang!"

CHAPTER SIX

*Y*ou know what's not cute? Free falling through the sky as your happy web gets ripped away from you like a bandage that was plastered across your fucking soul.

My heart hurts, my head hurts, everything hurts. On top of that, my wings are fluttering around like the pancakes I had for breakfast and I can't control the bastards. What good are these things if I can't use them? I know they're pretty and all, but hell, I actually think I'm going to fall to my death here.

My four Sun Gods are keeping their distance, free-falling faster than I am, though a lot more gracefully. Are they expecting me to simply spread my wings and soar through the sky? Highly unlikely, because they were sawn off when I was a goddamn child, and before then I wasn't allowed outside with them. The fuckers have no idea how to fly! They're one hundred percent *useless*! Pretty, but useless.

Fuck!

Tears prick at my eyes, and I know it's not from all the air rushing at my face—it's because my heart is properly broken.

After everything I've been through, this pain is the most tormenting.

I scream into the wind, fists clenched as I bellow my frustrations to the air rushing past me; the velocity whipping my voice away as fast as I can expel it.

Resigning myself to my fate, I flip onto my back, allowing my wings to cradle me as I curl into a tight, feathery cannonball.

Maybe this won't be such a bad way to die … at least I won't see the ground coming up to grab me. It'd probably be like falling asleep, but permanently.

Plummeting to my inevitable doom, I think I glimpse a swathe of red feathers through the clouds overhead …

Squinting, I realise it was more than likely a figment of my imagination, but it reminds me that there are still fuckers out there, just like the savage, red winged legionnaires, who would do damage to my girls.

Goddammit. Fucking conscience. Who's going to be there for them, if not me?

Snap out of it, Dell. Now!

I slap myself, just to make sure I'm getting the fucking message.

Flipping back over, I notice the ground is swiftly approaching. I wave my hands around at my disobedient Gods, making desperate faces, but they just make encouraging expressions and wave.

Fucking hell. These dicks. The least Kal could do is leave my happy web on while I careen to my death … flying lesson my arse.

"Flap, bitches," I scream, but they don't respond. Or can't. Probably because they have no muscle build-up. Hell, they'd probably snap in half if they stretched out at the speed I'm falling. How shit would that be? Get two pretty, new wings only to break them the second time I try to fly. And I'm sure as hell not jumping into that bog again! I still smell like the world's rotten bowels from our last group field trip.

I try a different approach.

"Please, girls," I plead.

Nothing.

My gods are clapping and punching the air. Do they really think I've got this?

"*Guys*! I actually don't know how to work these things!" In desperation I start flapping my arms.

Apparently, and at long last, they realise the seriousness of the situation and launch for me at the same time— colliding mid-air, stumbling over each other, pushing and shoving to get to me while I continue to plummet to my death.

Drake takes the opportunity to pummel his fist into Sol's perfect jawline, and Aero's on Kal's back, hauling at his wings trying to rein him like a horse.

Of course.

After everything I've been through, *this* is how I'm going to die, and all because my four fucking Sun Gods are too busy fighting over me to notice I'm about to go splat.

I say my final prayer to the world as the ground comes at me faster than a whore hell bent on survival, but just as I'm about to perish, my wings decide it's a great time to show up to the party—grabbing the wind and floating me down gently enough so that when I *do* go splat, I don't actually die. I still end up with a face full of sand, but that's the least of my worries as four sets of feet land around me.

Or should I say ... the least of *their* worries.

My beast has cracked her eye open, but I rein the bitch in, because this ... *I've* fucking got this.

Slowly, I uncurl, wiping the sand from my face and coughing up a few bugs that must've flown into my mouth while I was screaming up there. I push my tangled mass of hair from my face, run my hands over my dress, straighten, and look at Kal.

"*You!*" I point to him. At least he has the decency to look somewhat guilty. "This was *your* idea. You're in the sin bin!" He dishes me a moody frown he doesn't deserve to wear. I swivel before my beast jumps forward and wipes the frown clean off his face with her cock-biting teeth.

I'm facing Aero, and though my vagina is making cute little grabby hands, I'm fucking not. "*You* agreed to his plan, so you're in there too, along with my vagina who's got her panties in a twist because you're both on the naughty list. She *really* wanted your giant penises. Just saying. Your loss." I stomp my foot in the sand to emphasise my valid point. "Go home and think about what you've done!"

Aero blinks rapidly at me, probably trying to work out which head to think with. He takes a small step forward and I fucking hiss at him.

He takes a big step back. Go me.

I turn again, now facing Sol. I look the fucker square in the eye, even as my wings try to stroke the bastard. Frowning at the rogue tarts, I give them a little slap. They're totally killing my vibe right now.

"*You!*" I stab my finger into the centre of Sol's wide fucking chest. "You're a sadistic prick! You've got some serious grovelling to do if you want me to *ever* respect you again! I'm not sure if I can forgive you for what you did … I'm not sure I even want to try." I slap my wayward fucking wing again, for running her feathers along his face. "My wings are in the sin bin, and so are you, for being a straight *cunt.*"

He pales. Perhaps he recognised something wicked and feral in my eyes, but I don't give a single shit. I know what he saw and he deserved it because he *fucked up*. I'm leaving it to him to work out how he's going to make it up to me—if he can even be bothered, that is. Maybe he's too selfish to care.

I turn to Drake, levelling him with my furious gaze. "*And you*!"

He nods, uncertainty creasing his brow.

"Take me home. Please."

He exhales, visibly relieved.

"I'm exhausted and I need something to eat. And at *least* one orgasm before I sleep."

Brows raised, he smirks at the others who growl, fists clenched.

I give the three Gods who are in the naughty corner a final look over. "If *any* of you turn up without my permission, I'll be the proud owner of three giant, petrified penises."

I take Drake's hand and he flashes us into the Bright.

That's how it's fucking done.

CHAPTER SEVEN

I'm eating the best meal of my life, sitting across the table from my God of Dusk … who keeps looking at me like I'm an injured marsupial. It's really killing my vibe.

"*What?*" I ask for the tenth time in as many minutes. I'm buttering a piece of delicious looking corn toast that I'd like to eat in blissful ignorance. Just like Sap over there in the corner devouring her pile of dead animals in perfect fucking peace. She burps loudly, letting out a small plume of fire that would probably set the room ablaze if it wasn't carved from a sandstone mountain. She gives a little shake, throws herself into the air and takes off out the window.

Oh, to have that freedom …

Drake draws a deep breath. "Dell …"

I roll my eyes.

"Don't roll your eyes, this is important. We can't keep slipping shit under the rug, babe. That's what caused you to fall apart in the first place."

I whirl my hand, gesturing that we should move the fuck on, but apparently he doesn't get the fucking picture because in the next instant he's behind me, holding my wrists. "Dell,

66

please." He brings his mouth in close to my ear. "I'll reward you with orgasms …"

Hmmm … corn toast or orgasms? I tilt my head back and look up at him. "Okay."

Drake scoffs, looking way too fucking surprised. "Wow … that was easy."

"Don't speak too soon. What do you want to talk about?"

He pulls out a seat and sits down, facing me, resting his elbows on his knees. My wing curls around and strokes his arm. He raises an eyebrow and I shrug. "Ignore the tart, she has no concept of personal space."

"Right, I'll … try." He clears his throat. "Dell, I need to know where you stand with all this, how you're feeling. You've been through some shit."

I nod. "I guess I have."

He watches me, perhaps expecting more. I watch him back. The silence stretches out, consuming the room and becomes uncomfortable. Finally, he holds his palms out, fingers splayed. "That's it? That's all you've got?"

I go back to buttering my toast. "What do you want from me? To relive all the fuckery I've experienced in my life?" I shake my head. "No, thanks. I don't know if you've noticed but I'm really good at putting up walls. Can't we just work around them?"

He grasps my wrist again, preventing me from buttering that last corner of toast.

I frown … it really fucking irks me.

"I don't want to work *around* them, Dell. I want in. I don't care how fucked up it is behind those walls, I want it all. I want to *know* you. I want to help you *through* it."

I shake my head, snatching back my hand and buttering that last little corner. Now, if I could just eat it in peace … "I'm fine, Drake."

He turns my chair around so I'm facing him, making it

grind loudly. My wings jump in fright, then settle down in a permanently fluffed up state, enjoying the attention. Fucking hussies.

He takes my toast from my hand and sets it out of reach with his long God arm.

I sigh. He's on a sure path straight to the sin bin, and that'll be a real shame. No orgasms for me.

"You're not fine, and stop fucking dodging me. The others might be accepting of it but I won't fall for that shit. If you thought by coming here I was going to go easy on you, then you better think again."

Fuck me, he's hot when he gets all commanding like this.

"I care about you, Dell, I fucking do. And I will *not* sit by and watch your mind deteriorate. I know you've got a wall up, I know you don't feel shit the way regular people do and I understand why, but I also know that sometimes shit slips through the cracks." He's holding me by the shoulders in a firm grip that's got my vagina all roused and ready.

"You can't always wear this armour. What if it gets ripped away suddenly? You'd be fucked. If Kal hadn't put that happy web on you after—" He looks away briefly, then pulls me closer, gazing at me intently. "I could feel the pain your heart was going through. Kal won't always be there ... *we* might not always be there. I need you to have the tools to deal with this shit yourself, and I won't be able to relax until you do."

I pinch the bridge of my nose and close my eyes, sighing deeply. This shit's too heavy for a lunchtime meal. "You want to know my hard limits? My triggers?"

He pulls my hand from my face and tilts my chin so I'm looking him in the eyes. "Yes, that's a good start. A mind map so I can understand, and support you through the hard bits."

Why the fuck did I choose to go with the emotional analyser? I should've gone with Sol. I know he really screwed up and all, but I could've just set up camp in the kitchen and avoided him altogether. At least he repels the emotional bullshit, just like me. A good pair for sweeping stuff under the rug.

Drake's got that look in his eye that makes me feel like he wants to conquer me. I remind myself that he feeds off control, and, well … I guess I'm a bit of a loose unit.

"And then you'll give me orgasms?"

He nods. "As many as you want."

"Good, because I'm going to need hundreds after this shit. Now, give me my fucking corn toast."

He lifts a brow, but I just lay my hand out, waiting for my toast to be placed in my motherfucking palm so I have something to do with myself while I talk about this stupid shit.

With a low growl that's a bit fucking unnecessary, he hands me my toast and I take a small bite, avoiding his eye contact. "I don't like having my scar touched. I know I kept it and all, but just don't finger it. I felt everything when that knife went in, when they scooped me out and made me infertile. Touching it makes me feel that all over again."

I take another bite of my toast, chew slowly, and swallow. "Since we're kind of on the subject, I don't like having my toes played with. I know that's not the sort of shit you're after, but you asked."

He nods. "No toe jobs. It's a shame, but I think I can live with that."

I almost smile. "And I don't like feeling trapped, like I have no way out. I spent years trapped in a small dark box where I was fucked into oblivion every day, and now I don't cope well. Same goes for if I'm being smothered, I get anxious."

"Okay," he nods tentatively. "We can work through that …"

"Also …" I look out the window, focusing on the clouds scudding across the azure sky. "I've done a lot of fucking, yes, but I've never actually had consensual sex. Always brutal, always rough, but never because I asked for it. Or wanted it. So I developed my own way of coping … I had to in order to survive. I learnt to like it rough; the rougher, the more brutal, the better. I even told myself that it wasn't me having these sick desires—that it was someone else entirely. It made it easier to … well, swallow."

I smile, shrugging a shoulder, though I get no response from my stoic Dusk God. I smooth my features, clear my throat and continue. "In the end, I could only orgasm when they were fucking me so hard it felt like I would split."

I hear the breath catch in his throat.

I know it's dirty, I know it's fucked up, but he wanted to know. I'm done with caring if it makes them think differently of me.

"I found a way to enjoy it, to make it all seem better in my mind. If I didn't, I would've died a long time ago. Was I hiding?" I nod. "Perhaps, but I was alone, Drake. I had nobody but myself, with no place to call home, and nowhere to seek shelter from the fucked-up world we live in. All the while I was anchored by a memory that made me feel utterly responsible."

I look down at my toast, my appetite quickly disintegrating. "For the first four years of my life, my mother hid me. I barely went outside, never truly getting the chance to stretch my wings. She filled me with pure goodness, but then she … hurt me, and was taken from me, leaving me to question what was real and what was not." I clear my throat to ease the lump that's building there. "Kroe found me roaming the streets and I was thrown into the darkness, taught the meaning of brutal and mistaught the meaning of love. I grew up thinking there was no light in the world, Drake, though I tried to find it … to fight for it, because I so desperately wanted to believe that what my Mummy showed me was *real*. That her kisses, her hugs … were *real*."

I turn to look him in the eye, ignoring his pale tone and shadowed eyes, because I owe him this final piece. "When I threw myself off that cliff, I was going to a better place. I truly believed that. I thought, perhaps, despite our brutal parting, I was going back to the only person in my life who had shown me true love."

He looks like I just broke his golden fucking God heart, but I'm not quite done.

"But the most fucked up thing about all this? Women are taught that we aren't worthy of love. That we're only worth what our bodies can provide. If you have a vagina, you're objectified from the moment you exit the womb. What sort of life is that? One where I've become so desensitised to men pounding away at me, that I need it rough to get off? One where the only hope for shelter, was to hide in the shaded corners of my mind? One where I clung to the love of a man who sold my body for a living? One where we are slowly hacked away at, body and soul, until all that's left is the means to *fuck* us?" I nod, more to myself than to him. "So, yes —I have fucking walls, because I see *everything*. I forget *nothing*. I remember the face of every man who tortured me. I remember every instance someone called me a cunt, a whore, or a cum dumpster; and since I was four I've known there hasn't been a goddamn thing I could do to change it, because I'm a *female*. Because I was a Lesser Fae whore with no uterus and no fucking worth."

Tossing my toast down, I stand, shoving my chair back.

I need to get out of here.

Walking swiftly towards the door, I ignore the fact that

my wings are trying to coax me back to Drake. I don't know where I'm going, but my heart feels like it's about to explode out of my chest and I'm shaking all over.

He's suddenly in front of me, with his golden fucking wings out, breathing so deeply I can hear the blood pumping through his veins.

"What do you want from me now?" My voice sounds whiny, like I'm pleading, but I've had enough. I hold out my trembling hands. "See? I have nothing more to give!"

He takes a step closer, brushing his hand past my cheek and around the back of my head; threading his fingers through my curls. He jerks me forward, lifting my chin, arching my neck … and locks me into a fierce kiss.

His tongue cleaves between my teeth, seeking dominance over the mouth that just spoke the harsh words of my brutal existence, slandering this pitiful world that's partly his own.

He doesn't seem to care.

The realisation is like a trigger, and I arch my body against him, my wings curling around and rubbing his glorious golden ones. I explore the rivets and swells of his pectorals, running my fingertips along to the hollow at the base of his neck, so tantalisingly smooth …

Drake drops his hands to my thighs, parting my legs while lifting me up and wrapping them around his waist. The short shift I'm wearing inches upwards, and he holds me against his body by the blooms of my arse, walking me back to the wall and pressing me against it.

He pulls away from my mouth, careful not to graze me with his lengthened canines, though I wouldn't mind if he shed a little blood … "I'm going to show you *exactly* what you've been missing out on."

Holy fucking Dusk babies …

"Put your hands above your head."

"Like this?" I raise my hands, fingers entwined.

"Perfect."

He presses into me, using his hips to hold me in place, and I mould my body against the massive, throbbing erection placed conveniently between my legs. My vagina's so damn excited, she's pretty sure she's about to get the chance to give him a gold vagina star right on his penis. Maybe she's being presumptuous, but a vagina can hope.

He rips the dress from my body and his hungry gaze drops to the place they tore my uterus from me—an ugly red scar, crooked, thick and long, owning the entire lower half of my abdomen. "I'm glad you kept it." His eyes roam back up my body in a slow, languid stroke, settling on my gaze, both hooded and carnal. "That scar tells the story of a woman whose beauty goes far deeper than her skin's surface. It tells the story of a woman whose *perfection* lies within her *imperfections*."

I'm holding my breath, torn between running away or devouring this man whole.

"I'm going to fucking *worship* your body."

Well ... fuck.

Devour him it is.

He pulls his top off and lets it fall to the ground, his steady, sizzling gaze teasing. I crave to touch him, to run my hands down the exquisite, chiselled length of his torso. I lower my hands but he grasps them in his own, returning them to their place above my head.

He lowers me, hooks his thumbs into the waistband of his pants, and with a small sultry smile, tugs them down. Stepping out of them, he moves closer—our breaths shared and gazes locked. His manhood strains between us. I look down and ...

Fuck me.

The sight of his oversized erection almost makes me go floppy.

"Dell, look at me."

I gulp. "I am."

"Not there." He laughs and tilts my face so I'm looking into his eyes. "Here."

"Okay," I whisper. "But ..."

"You're okay, Dell. Everything is going to be okay. Just don't stop looking at me. Do you understand?"

I nod.

He runs his thumb beneath the seam of my panties, at the sensitive part of my hip and I gasp, biting my lower lip.

"Can I remove your underwear?"

"Yes," I groan, aching, desperate to take his hair in my hands ... to grind his face against my throbbing bud that's practically screaming with anticipation.

He tugs and my panties shred like tissue paper.

I'm *entirely* exposed to this man ... to the heat of his cock, the smell of his desire, the urgent beat of his heart meeting my own.

He leans into me, bringing his lips to my ear, his breath hot against my quickening pulse. "I can smell you. You're so fucking wet for me."

I gasp, arching my head back, desperate for his touch, my hungry gaze falling to the throbbing vein on his neck, just below his ear ...

I run my tongue over my lips and swallow.

"Hungry, babe?"

"Starving."

Smirking, he picks me up, wrapping my legs around his waist. He dips his head, looks up at me through thick lashes and flicks my nipple with the tip of his tongue. I cry out from the sensual tickle.

He retreats, smiles, then returns ... this time taking my nipple into his mouth, gently sucking and flicking the peak with his tongue, sending warm jolts of pleasure straight to my love bud.

Heat gathers, the beginnings of an orgasm … a quivering flame brightening. Again, he retreats, watching me, holding me in orgasmic limbo as he shows my nipples the attention they deserve.

"Not yet babe, not yet."

He lowers his mouth to my other breast, licking and sucking while he massages my exposed nipple with the pad of his thumb. I grind my hips, seeking friction and brush against his pulsing manhood, gasping as waves of heat wash over me.

He takes my hands, kissing each palm, and places them on his shoulders while edging me higher so that his cock is positioned at the aching entrance to my wetness.

Shifting my hips, I press my opening against him, hissing a sharp gasp. "You're … you're huge …"

"It's okay, babe … you're ready." His face is all hard lines, voice serious. "I won't hurt you. If you want it, it's yours."

Rubbing against him, I caress the beautiful ache of my clit against his shaft, closing my eyes, the fire building as Drake tantalises me with gentle wisps of his magic.

"Look at me, Dell."

I groan, open my eyes and stare at him, barely able to focus.

He shifts his hips and pulls his dick away from me, the warm tickle of magic disappearing from my tender bud. "What are you doing?" I pant, outrage staining my words.

He lifts a brow. "Do not close off from me, understand?"

"I …" fucking hell. "Okay."

"Eyes open," he says, wrapping his hand around the side of my face and stroking my cheek with his thumb.

Our gazes locked, he gently pulls me back onto him so that I'm straddling his shaft, my folds slick with desire. He takes my face in both his hands, caresses my lips, my neck. "When you're ready, ease yourself onto me."

I've never been asked to ease myself onto *anything*, let alone a penis.

My beast cracks an eye open. Perhaps she likes the fact that this man is relinquishing some of his control to me ...

I drop my hips slightly so that the head of his cock is perched at my wet, throbbing entrance. I ease forward and the tip of his shaft enters me, sending waves of pleasure up my channel, causing me to cry out; wanting, *needing* to take all of him in.

"I don't want to miss a single fucking moment of this," he groans, twisting his fingers through my hair, holding our eye contact. "Do you know how fucking *perfect* you are?"

I relax, whimpering, open myself to him further, feeling the firm press of his length as he fills me entirely, the base of his shaft pushing against the sensitive outer shell of my woman cave.

"Fuck, Dell ..." His lips crash into mine, claiming my mouth, sucking my lower lip between his teeth and holding onto it.

Slowly, carefully, he begins to move—gently at first, gaining momentum until he's thrusting his full, delicious length into me. I tangle my hands around his neck, through his hair; running them across his back, his ass, and around his cock that's wet with my arousal.

I take his fingers, slick with my desire, and slip them in my mouth—slide my tongue across them and watch his eyes ignite, glazed with lust.

My fire's building ... I can taste it.

Sense it.

Smell it.

I've never felt so free, never needed anything as much as I do *this*.

It's not forced, it's not a desperate plea for survival.

It's certainly not a lie.

It's raw.

It's real.

It feels *right*.

I lunge for his mouth—kissing, sucking, exploring every luscious curve. My beast gains a little purchase and nips at his lip … it's not enough to draw blood, but intentional, even so.

"Fuck …" I lash her back into her confines and stare at his lip, at the small swelling, wanting as much to split it open as to lick and suck and kiss the redness away.

My beast snarls, thrashing against my restraints.

Drake has paused, seated inside me, watching me with dark, smouldering intensity. "It's okay, babe." He pushes the hair from my eyes, tilting my head with decisive power. "I want her ... I want all of you."

I shake my head. "You don't know what she's capable of. She might hurt you."

He thrusts again, plunging into me with force. I let out a strangled groan, relishing the feel of him so deeply embedded; the full length of him swathed in my pulsing cocoon. He pulls out slowly, then renews the action, again and again, watching me with a heated gaze. "I'm hoping she does," he whispers, his voice hoarse, heavy with desire.

My beast licks her lips, ready to pounce.

And yet I hold her back.

"Let her go." He thrusts again, his throbbing cock, thick and hard, filling me entirely.

My beast is screaming, clawing at the air …

"I want all of you, babe." He nips at my lip.

"The dark ..." *thrust.*

"The light …" *thrust.*

"Every shade in-between …" *thrust.*

"Let her *fucking* go!"

With a feral roar my beast pounces.

We lunge at him—pulling him harder into ourselves, working our body up and down his shaft in perfect harmony to the rhythm of our own fucking symphony. We take his hands, pushing them onto our breasts. He tweaks and pulls, drawing them into his mouth one by one, sucking and flicking until they're hard, flaming peaks, tingling and aching at once.

Harder and harder we thrust, the pulsating bud of our clit perfectly positioned, sliding along the full length of his cock.

He pulls us from the wall and we throw our head back, arching our neck and revelling in the feel of his canines sliding along the base of our throat, feeding our swelling orgasm.

I'm not stupid, I know what she's doing.

My beast is submitting herself to Drake.

Fucking hell.

"Do it …" we plead, needing those teeth to pierce our skin more than we've ever needed *anything* before in our fucked-up life.

We feel the pressure against our carotid artery—understand the amount of control he's showing by preventing those canines from piercing our skin.

"Do it, Drake …"

He retreats and, losing patience, we lunge forward—grabbing handfuls of golden hair and tug his head to the side. We pull off, letting the swollen tip of his cock sit poised at our entrance.

We smile against his pounding pulse for a second … two … then drive our hips against him, taking him fully, at the same time sinking our teeth right into his fucking neck.

I haul my beast back into place, wanting a front row seat

as blood seeps from the wound, pooling on my tongue, sending my senses wild.

Holy Dusk God, he tastes good … like his blood was *meant* for me.

He groans, arms tightening their hold, fists clenching at my hair while I ride his cock, moaning into his neck, swallowing his blood like the animal I am.

My eyes roll into the back of my head, my wings extending to their full glory as we cling to each other; pounding hard and fast, riding the surging waves. I fall over that edge, wings sinking into my back as the orgasm tears through my body in thick, throbbing waves.

I scream my release, my teeth untangling themselves from his flesh, as Drake dips his head into the crook of my neck then sinks his canines into my yearning flesh.

It's an ecstatic, piercing pain, lulled by the soft flick of his tongue caressing the wounds he just made.

Crushing us together, he finds his release—hot spurts of seed filling me as I cry out—a golden warmth saturating my heart, claiming a corner that was empty and cold.

Drake pulls those teeth from my neck then kisses at the sore so fucking delicately. "Mine," he whispers against the sensitive skin. It pebbles beneath his breath and he envelopes me in his glorious wings, holding me to him, caressing my face.

Well … fuck.

That happened.

A flash of light lands us in his bedroom. He reverently lowers me onto the bed, his body stretched above me— allowing me the perfect vision of my Dusky Sun God.

"She accepted me." He runs a finger around my lips, making them tingle. "*You* accepted me."

I feel the tether inside myself—the golden link, clinging to my heart like its life depends on it.

Yeah, I just formed a mating bond with a fucking Sun God.

I'm not sure what this means for my internal walls, but my vagina's so goddamn proud of herself, trying to take all the credit.

Back down, twat. For once, this was my own doing.

CHAPTER EIGHT

"You're very quiet …" Drake's running his fingers through my hair, a crease forming between his eyes.

I am, only because I'm cradling that golden tether like it's a newborn baby, which is strange, but I just can't seem to stop.

"I can feel you in here …" I tap my chest and he nods, smiling.

"I can feel you, too. You're right where you belong."

His words make me beam, but then I'm struck with a harrowing realisation. "I'm sorry I didn't get a chance to preen my feathers for you beforehand," I say seriously.

He quirks a coy smile. "Don't worry, babe. I got the message loud and clear when you started salivating over the sight of my neck."

I slap him playfully on his chest. "I did not!"

"Actually, you did. It was hot as fuck. I could have taken you right there and then. Points to me for being a gentleman."

That was very gentlemanly of him, I have to admit. The thought makes me so happy that I start to ... cry?

"Dell?" Drake shuffles into a sitting position and hauls me up, so I'm straddling the sexy bastard and his taut abdominals, which makes me cry harder. With tender hands, he wipes away my tears, watching me with a face etched in concern. "Babe, what's wrong?"

"I just ... I just ... *I don't know!*" Overcome with emotion, I wail, tears streaming down my face, my breathing ragged.

He lifts a brow and ... starts to fucking *laugh?*

"What are you laughing at?" I sob scream.

Clearing his throat, he tugs me into his chest. "Nothing, nothing at all. I'm sorry."

"Good, because I'm really moody right now, okay? I don't need your sass." I gulp, trying to swallow my tears.

He looks confused, and a little cautious. "That came on quick ..."

"Oh, really?" I challenge, pulling away.

He puts his hands up like he's surrendering, which is good; if he looks at me strangely again, I might just scratch his fucking face off.

"Okay, I'll keep my laughter to a minimum." He strokes my hair, like I'm a fucking lap dog.

Actually, it feels amazing and I nuzzle at his chest to encourage the action.

"You like that, don't you babe?"

I nod into his chest, hiccupping. "Yes (hiccup) I fucking ... (hiccup) do (hiccup)."

"Was there anything else bothering you?"

"Not (hiccup) really." Just my overwhelming emotions. Though, now that he mentions it, my other three Sun Gods are probably going to be *pissed* that I chewed on Drake's neck. They may be in my sin bin, but I don't want them to stay in there forever ...

He tugs at my hair so my chin tilts up, exposing my face to him wholly. I'm not sure what he sees, but he frowns, and I really want to trace that little crease mark between his eyes with my tongue.

"Dell?"

Okay, concentrate. "Won't the others be mad we mated?" I blurt out. Fucking word vomit, but I'm kind of being led by my emotions right now.

He smiles and it's so dazzling that I want to jump the bastard … and cry again. Probably at the same time. What the hell is wrong with me?

"Mad that I got accepted first? Probably. Not my fault they fucked up."

"Accepted … first? What do you mean?" I'm being coy with my words because I'm not sure where Drake stands with all of this—he *did* say he's not one to share.

He shrugs, though a half smile is curling one corner of his mouth. "I'm privy to your body's sensations, Dell. I know they make you feel good."

"Ahhh …" Yeah, fuck. Nothing like your new 'mate' knowing you've got a thing for three other Sun Gods. Awkward.

"I'm not saying I fucking like it, or that it's going to be easy, but I've had a while to get used to this. Especially since we saw your wings, the prophecy—"

"What's that supposed to mean?"

He shakes his head, rubbing at his face with his hand. "Sorry, fuck, I'm so tired I'm rambling about crap that's not important right now. I'm just glad I got my venom in there first, that you accepted *me* first. That's something we'll always have."

I'm pretty sure my Sun God boyfriend just gave me permission to bone other Sun Gods. I thought this was going to be a lot more complicated.

Awww … I feel myself getting teary again. I draw in a deep lung-full of his scent and almost orgasm on the spot. "Fuck, you smell good." I guess that's one way to keep this emotional see-saw at bay.

I feel his smile as he kisses me on the top of my head. "So do you. I've loved your scent from the moment I met you on that fucking cliff. It was an effort not to bite that pretty little neck of yours even then."

I smile at that, whiffing his chest again so I don't burst into tears. "Savage."

"Always."

A sudden pain grips my insides, the sensation similar to when my uterus was sliced from my fucking abdomen. I curl into myself, arching off Drakes glorious body and moaning like the whore I … was. "Fucking shit cunt …" I grind through my teeth.

Drake shifts me sideways so he can see my face. "What's wrong?"

My insides are deteriorating at a rapid fucking rate, that's what's wrong. "I think I'm *dying*."

He rubs circles on my back, somehow managing to add to my discomfort. "You are in a lot of pain, I agree … you're immortal though, babe. It's not possible for you to just randomly die anymore, unless you're mortally wounded."

"Yeah well, I beg to fucking differ, because I'm pretty sure I'm dying," I hiss, as another wave of pain threatens to explode my guts all over the bedroom.

Drake shifts me off him, grabs the linen throw off the end of the bed and wraps it around me as I breathe through the pain, rocking into myself and trying to picture happier times when I wasn't dying from the inside out.

"What can I do to help?"

"I don't fucking know! You're the God!"

Something dribbles down the inside of my thigh, and my

eyes snap open. Fuck, I think I just peed myself. Wait, the pain's easing … did I just *pass something*?

I wiggle off the bed and dash past my overbearing Dusk God, determined to make it to the bathroom before he smells the wee.

"I thought you were dying? Where the fuck are you going?"

"Toilet. Don't come in."

"Fucking heard that one before. I thought we agreed, no walls!"

I slam the door to the washroom closed. "I'm allowed a fucking bathroom wall, you sicko!"

I drop the throw, look down, and immediately spot the blood dribbling down my leg. "Shiiiiit …"

Drake bangs on the door. "I smell blood … what's going on in there?"

Good fucking question. I swipe my finger through the blood and inspect it closely. "I think my insides are falling out through my vagina …"

"I'm coming in." The door starts to open.

"No, don't!" I squeal, trying to wrap myself in the throw again, like a neat little blood parcel, but it's pretty ineffective at such short notice.

He's standing at the door, naked and glorious, nostrils flaring, sniffing the air. He takes a tentative step closer, his oversized soldier perking right the hell up.

"Fuck …"

I try *really* hard to avoid looking at his penis, which is making me think randy thoughts. I also try to avoid the internal glow of that golden tether, that has a goddamn aura around it now.

He sniffs the air again, takes another two tentative steps towards me, reaches his arm out like I have the fucking plague, and rips the throw straight from my body.

I let out a squawk and pounce back, ineffectively covering my nether regions with spread hands. Drake stares at the blood dribbling down my legs, then sniffs a few more times, long and hard.

"Are you fucking *smelling* me right now?" I screech. I know I threw away my dignity a long time ago, but this really is next level.

Drake goes pale and takes a step *away* from me.

Whatever I have, it must be contagious.

Fuck.

"Are your organs about to start falling out through your genitals, too?" I screech.

Typical. I mate with a Sun God, then kill the bastard.

"That's not your organs, babe. You're in heat."

Pfft. "Fuck off, you're lying to me."

He lifts a brow, his cock twitching at the same time. So synchronised … it makes me want to bury said cock right into the throes of my vagina where he can pump his Dusk juice to his heart's content, smothering my insides in all that fertile godliness …

Ahhh … shit.

"What the fuck does that even mean? Like a female dog?" My voice is cutting in and out—I'm having a minor panic attack. No big deal. I guess my mood swings make perfect bloody sense now.

Fucking hormones, making me look like a pussy.

He puts his hands up, as if to placate my erratic outburst. "Kind of, except it happens more regularly for us, even more so for a Lesser. You bleed a little when your body reaches its peak fertility period. Did nobody ever explain this to you?"

"No!" I scream, realising I'm acting unreasonably but carrying on anyway. "Because we weren't allowed to talk! I bled a couple of times, but it never felt like this … and then my uterus got cut out, remember? I have no uterus! I have the scar to prove it!" I point at said fucking scar, which Drake only glances at momentarily before he runs his hand through his hair, still eyeing the blood that's dribbling down my leg.

"Doesn't seem that way, babe …"

I stare at him like he's insane, though the grim reality of my newfound fertility slowly starts to sink in. I chew my nails, because I'm in fucking *heat*. And I have four Sun Gods my wings and vagina have taken a liking too, and one rogue uterus who wants to bathe in their semen cocktails.

He frowns, rubbing his chin. "This complicates things a bit."

I stare blankly at him. "A *bit*? That's a fucking understatement. Birth control?" At this stage, I'm getting pretty desperate. A week of heat if a dog's anything to go by, with no Sun God penetration? At least I can still have wingasms, I guess. And Drake's magic ones …

Okay, maybe it's not *so* bad. Unless my beast cuts loose again and bites another Sun God, which will probably lead to more erratic fornicating. What a disaster.

Drake takes a step closer. "Birth control? Not one hundred percent reliable."

"Fucking swell."

"Your fertile stage only lasts for seventy-two hours or so … usually."

"Well, at least that's something." A week is a long time when you have four Sun Gods you want to bang. Three days doesn't seem so bad. Still, I close my eyes, trying to breathe through the anxiety my uterus has stirred with all her cum-calling.

"Though, I'm not good at sharing."

"And you're not good at sharing." I snap my eyes open, eyeing a swiftly approaching paternal Dusk God. I put my hands up as meagre protection, watching his massive appendage bounce to the beat of his strides.

"Wait. Drake … woah, let's take a metaphorical step back here!" I literally take a step back—into the wall.

Shit.

"I know you're a clucking, fucking rooster, but I've had about two seconds to come to terms with the fact that I *have* a uterus … *two seconds.*"

He boxes me in, his hands pressing into the wall either side of me, wings manifesting. "Do you want kids, Dell?"

My wings come out, pushing me forward and shoving me into Drakes horizontal cock, which, with nowhere else to go, pops up between us, all perky and hopeful.

Fuck you Wings, keep your opinions to yourselves.

Drake raises a brow, quirking a labia-eating smile at me.

"Well that's a loaded question if I've ever heard one." Mainly because I can't bloody lie.

Drake runs a finger over one of my feathers and a shiver runs through my body, straight to my vagina. That golden tether starts to pulse with light. "Answer me, Dell. Do you?"

Fucking Dusk God, he knows my wings have a thing for him. I swat his petting hand away. "Yes, okay? Happy now? I've fantasised about it, wished I could do it, but that's not the point, Drake!"

His smile grows and he pins me to the wall with his hips. "I saw it first, I call dibs. Fuck if I'm sharing your uterus with any of those fuckers for at least a year."

"Whoa horsey, whoa. My mother hacked my wings off with a hand saw then doused me in flammable liquid and set me on fire. I'm not sure I'm mummy material. I'd probably make a shit parent, know what I mean? We're *not* rushing into this." I'm saying this but at the same time, I'm grinding up against him like a rogue whore in heat … which is exactly what I am. Fucking touché.

He grabs me under the chin, tilting my head to give him direct access to my mouth. "That's fine babe, I won't rush you." He kisses me with a hard, possessive edge and pulls back, his lips a hair's breadth from mine. "But I *am* calling dibs."

My beast has her eyes open and my wings are getting all up in his pretty face. I'm surprised he isn't swatting them away. I wish mine were as well behaved as his.

He kisses his way down the side of my neck, over the puncture marks—paying them extra attention, like they're some kind of rare treasure.

My skin prickles. He's being so gentle, yet so fucking firm. I edge my way up, stand on my tiptoes so that I'm perched at the tip of his engorged penis …

Fuck me, I *need* him in me right now.

"I want to spread my seed through you—grow a mini manifestation of the way I feel for you …"

I close my eyes, moaning for his filthy words. "Fuck yes, talk dirty to me …"

I feel him smile against my neck. "I'm going to be there with you every step of the way, watching you grow with our child."

I'm wet. Hot damn. "I'm going to grow so round for you!" Fuck yes. I'm so good at talking dirty.

Drake licks my neck, slow and sensual. "I'll rub your cankles and feed you cake. I'm going to look after you so good, babe."

"Oh fuck, Drake. Keep talking like that while you fuck me against the wall."

He pulls back and my feet drop to the ground, just as I was about to clamber aboard his dick in a hormonal fucking heat trance.

"Fuck, sorry …" He takes a few steps backwards, putting space between me and my evil uterus.

It's an effort not to chase the bastard and launch myself at him vagina first. Ignoring my wayward wings that are reaching out to Drake like they want him to pick them up for a cuddle, I wipe at the sweat beading off my brow with the back of my hand. "No, no, it's fine."

It's not fine.

I'm randy as fuck. It turns out my uterus is *worse* than my fucking vagina—she's like her own little cheer squad, screaming for all the God jizz. She wants to roll around in it all day, every day.

Fuck me, I've got my work cut out for me with these two *and* my beast. It's a full-time job. I'm not sure I have time for babies too. "I think I need to sleep this off." I stare at the blood smeared over my legs. "Yeah, that's what I need."

Drake swallows thickly. "You need a bath, too. And you won't be able to sleep with your wings out. Orgasm first, bath afterwards? If you go and lay on the bed, I'll give you the orgasm from here."

I nod. "Seems like a well thought out plan that involves very little risk and maximum control."

He reaches down, grabs the blanket, and tosses it at me. "Wrap this around yourself so I don't launch myself at you when you walk past, pin you against the wall, and fuck you until my seed is dribbling down your legs."

Fucking hell. I shake my head, trying to wrap the blanket around me. It takes about ten minutes because I have to lure my unwilling wings into my safety cocoon, so they don't stroke at my Dusky horn dog on the way past him, then lead me straight onto his erect cock. It doesn't stop them from trying though, as I waddle past, white knuckled, straining to hold the blanket in place. I make it almost to the bed before the fabric is pulled from my hands and my wings unfurl in dramatic flair.

I sigh and clamber onto the bed—wings uncomfortably spread beneath me, legs splayed and forming a giant 'V' in the air.

Lifting my head from the bed, I peer at Drake between my legs.

He's frowning, fist between his teeth, eyeing the eager little party goer perched between my legs. "What are you doing, Dell?"

I thought it was obvious. "Giving you direct access to my love nest? I figure if you have a good view of her, then the orgasm will be even *better*."

He prowls towards me, eyes hooded, chest heaving. "I know what you're doing …"

"No, you don't."

"Really?" He cocks a brow, grabs my legs, and pushes them back together.

I'm repressing my thinly veiled disappointment that he didn't take my uterus's vagina bait, when he flips me over in one swift movement and pushes my legs apart, propping my hips up. Something warm, firm, and hard presses against my entrance …

"You want me to fuck you, don't you?"

"Drake …"

"*Answer me*."

Oooh yeah, growly tone …

My uterus is screaming in excitement, even though I'm gulping back muted emotions that make no sense. *Of course* this is what I want! And I might just start to cry if I don't get it *right now.*

I reach between my legs and rub my lady lips, causing Drake to groan his appreciation as he caresses my folds with the tip of his God rod—both of us working her at the same time … the slick sound making me drool in anticipation as I rock my hips in a smooth, rhythmic motion.

"Yes. I want you to fuck me, Drake. I want you to drown me in your seed." I scream in ecstasy as he sheaths his dick inside me, filling me deliciously in one swift motion.

It isn't gentle, but I don't want gentle right now.

I want hard.

I want fast.

I want him to lose his fucking control. Or ... my uterus does. But it's essentially the same thing ... kind of.

I'm practically brimming with him as he thrusts, threading his hands around my thighs, lifting my lower half from the bed and causing a slick, slapping sound to pulse through the room. "Is this what you want?"

"Oh God, just like that ..." I pant, hands kneading the sheets. "Don't stop."

His pace quickens, the pressure between my legs rising as he hits that throbbing sweet spot over and over again, while my clit receives a rhythmic kiss from his deep, guttural thrusts. "I'm close ..."

Fuck yes. Baby making time ...

My uterus rubs her little hands together then closes her eyes, waiting to be doused in Drake's fertile cream filling.

"Come for me ..."

His words undo me. I quiver in an explosion of pleasure as he wrings every last drop of orgasmic pleasure from my pulsing body. My wings sink into my back before he gently lowers me to the bed. He slips out of me, screaming his own release as warm ropes of precious Dusk jizz pour onto my back in spurts ...

What.

The.

Fuck.

With a satiated growl, he leans over me and kisses the side of my face.

"Ahh ... what the fuck was that?"

"What do you mean? That was me serenading your vagina the old-fashioned way." He hums a guttural growl into my ear, nipping at my lobe, and I almost swat the fucker in the nose with my fist.

"Did you just squirt your seed onto my back?"

"I figured you needed a bath anyway, so …"

"Why is it on my back and not coating the walls of my randy uterus?"

He sucks my lobe into his mouth and I have to fight to stay mad at the sensual bastard.

"You'll thank me in about seventy-one hours when your hormones are no longer running the show." He pushes himself up, grunts his appreciation of his handiwork with a goofy grin splitting his face, then slaps my fucking arse.

"Un-fucking-likely!" I arch my neck, looking over my shoulder at the creamy mess, all that precious baby batter drizzling onto the bed covers. "And now I'm covered in your jizz."

"You should always be covered in my jizz." He flashes away, then returns with a small hand towel which he uses to clean up his mess … a mischievous glint still caught in his eyes.

"I'm pissed."

He lifts me off the bed and plonks me on my feet, then steers me towards the washroom. "I can tell."

"My uterus is even more pissed."

He kisses me on the top of my head. "She'll forgive me, one day. When you're actually ready."

I reach the threshold, turn around, and slam the door in his face—only mildly aware that my hormones are turning me into a hot mess.

The ever-ready bath steaming in the corner looks inviting. I pad over to it, take the three descending steps into its warmth and instantly begin to relax. I dip my face below the water, run my fingers through my hair, and resurface, feeling like a woman re-born. Kind of like when I was dragged out of that bog, minus the shit smell.

I rest my head against the side and float my limbs to the surface, my nipples peeping up to say hello.

The moment of solitude, and distance from my tasty Dusk God, allows me a small reprise of clarity from my overbearing hormones.

Things are advancing swiftly …

I've got my other Gods to consider, who are likely still licking their wounds in the sin bin. I don't even know where they sit with all this … they may not be happy to share me with Drake.

"After I've had a nana nap, I think we need a group sex talk," I say, half to myself.

Yeah, we definitely need one of those.

Drake flashes into the room, standing by the far wall and wearing a look of piqued interest. "A *what?*"

Yeah, this is going to be really fucking interesting.

CHAPTER NINE

"*I*'m not wearing that." I point to the leather chastity belt dangling from Drake's hand.

"Babe, I'm not asking."

I glare at him. "Don't call me *babe* when you're swinging that thing at me."

He quirks a brow and takes a step closer—I take a step further away.

I wish my wings would leave him alone while he's waving that thing around. I know they're fanning for his ever-present erection, but they're really cramping my style. I frown at the tarts rubbing themselves all over his face.

"Look, Dell, it's to protect you from the others. Kal and Aero lack in the control department and I wouldn't put it past them to jump you on the spot when they smell you're in heat. It's just a precaution."

I take another step back. "That thing has 'drama' written all over it. I can just imagine what the others are going to say when I walk in for our sex talk wearing a fucking chastity belt, coated in your scent from our recent mating bonk."

He rolls his eyes, throwing his hands up, making the

chastity belt fling about dramatically. "I'll give you the fucking key!"

Key? Well then ... "Can I wear it around my neck like a trophy?"

He sighs, smiling, though he tries to hide it. His chin dimple always becomes more prominent when he's trying to be serious. "If it fucking pleases you, babe."

Nice. I like the thought of wearing the means to my vagina around my neck, owning it like the boss lady I am. "Is it pretty?"

He holds up the key and I gasp at its solid, ornate beauty —a golden hue of which I've never seen before. "Is that ... a different sort of gold?"

He nods. "Old gold forged from the Labian Mountains of the West. It's a tribute to the solemn respect placed on High Fae in heat."

I point at the chastity belt, scowling. "Use that thing often, do you? To protect all those High Fae bitches in heat from your randy God rod?"

"Calm down babe ..."

"Don't tell a High Fae in heat to calm down! Boy, do you have a lot to learn!"

He winces. "Look Dell, this thing's been hanging in a cupboard for thousands of years." He wipes a cobweb off the crotch, blushing. "As you can see, it hasn't had any use."

Oh ...

"Soooo, you don't have a harem of High Fae in heat, fanging for a chance to spawn a baby Dusk God? Clambering all over you, trying to get you to slip your cock into their sloppy, less than favourable vaginas?"

He rolls his eyes, shaking his head. "No Dell, I don't. You're it." He raises his hands. "Not that you have a sloppy, less than favourable vagina ..."

I throw him an evil glare. The fucker just grins and waves the key at me.

I fold my arms, head cocked. "Well then, I may not need to hew a piece of that sparkly floor at the Day Kingdom after all … I can wear my contingency plan around my neck!"

He nods, huffing. "Yeah … probably enough to buy you a nice little home in the East if you ever get sick of my dick. Anyway, it's yours for the keeping, if you'll just put this fucking thing on." He jingles the chastity belt.

I sigh. "Fine, but it better not chafe." I signal him permission to approach my fertile lady parts.

Taking a deep breath, he walks towards me, unbuckling the fastenings of the belt. I lift my shift and he quickly goes about securing the straps over top of my underwear.

I frown. "Are you holding your breath?"

He nods, looking up at me sheepishly.

"Does my vagina smell bad?"

He rolls his eyes and shakes his head.

"What then?"

Face reddening, cheeks bulging, he secures the last buckle and gives the whole thing a firm 'tug', then quickly steps back, gasping for air.

"I held my breath so I wouldn't smell you, be compelled to feast on you for dinner, then shoot a baby right up into that fresh little uterus of yours."

"Oh."

My vagina smells good then, go me! I wouldn't mind a 'good smelling vagina' badge.

He tugs a chain from his golden god wear and runs his fingers over the two ends, magically forming a latch that he threads the key along.

"That was fancy, I thought you just had your other trick?"

He shrugs and puts the chain around my neck, fastening it at the back then pulling my hair through. "Mainly. We can do other things but nothing too spectacular since our power started to dwindle, thanks to that bastard."

"Right." That bastard. Meaning my father, the man who killed my mother. "Of course."

Drake clasps my bare shoulders with his large, calloused hands. "Speaking of power, have you felt anything since you got your wings back? Given your … heritage, you should have some sort of gift. The king can mould his power in a lot of ways, though he isn't privy to our main abilities. We're all interested to see if you have the same … capabilities."

I fondle the key hanging between my breasts, thankful for the distraction. "Nope, nothing so far."

I shudder inwardly, the memory of feeling so helpless while I watched my mother get hacked up by my father painfully clear. Mum had asked me many times if I had ever felt a 'well of warmth' inside myself. I never did. And so, I watched her die, and there wasn't a damn thing I could do about it.

Perhaps he senses my awkwardness because he pulls me to him, the silence hanging between us. Finally, he draws in a deep, shuddering breath. "Okay. You ready to go?"

"Yup."

I couldn't save my mother. That's a scar I'll bear forever, knowing I could have prevented the one thing that might have turned the tides of history forever, if only I had the competency. Sure, I was only four, but Mum kept asking … this *well of warmth* must have been in me somewhere.

My biggest fear now is that something will happen to my Sun Gods. That I'll be, once again, forced to watch someone I love die at the hands of my father and be powerless to stop it.

I guess that's the risk I took when I began to open my heart to the four men who are trying to mend all the broken parts of me.

Drake flashes us to a giant, flat rock in the middle of the ocean, with a round stone table in the heart, surrounded by six tiny stools made of the same stone. Everything's drab and dreary. The place even *smells* solemn, like it doesn't know what it wants to be.

"It's really windy here," I state the obvious, pushing my tangle of wind-swept hair from my face.

Drake nods. "It's the one spot that has a foot in all four territories. Neutral ground."

Part of all four territories? Probably why this place smells so confused—like a petrified identity crisis. This place and I should get along just swell.

"Plus," he continues, "with the wind whipping your scent away, it should help everyone keep their cocks contained … hopefully."

I roll my eyes, only because my uterus told me to. She doesn't understand what's so bad about having a cocktail of Sun God jizz all up in her twat. Which is why it's me in charge, and not her.

I do a full spin. Yup, no way to get in, no way to get out— unless you have wings or the ability to 'flash' through the Bright, or whatever the fuck it is. Maybe they should leave me here until I work it all out for myself, then they wouldn't have to carry me around like a white feathery manny-pack.

The sea is swarming with circling megalodons, their giant fins cutting jagged paths through the choppy waves. "Is this their breeding ground?"

Drake notes my attention on the giant fucking sharks. "Yeah. It will take too much energy for Kal to deter their hunger, so you'll have to stay on the island this time, I'm afraid."

So rude.

"The others will be here soon, let's go take a seat."

"Did you send them a pigeon?"

He laughs. "Something like that. We're connected by the sun, all harnessing the same energy, so there's a bilateral current between us. Through it, we can receive abstract flickers of emotion or thought."

I nod like I know what the hell he's talking about. The only thing I've ever harnessed is a penis. I'm so underqualified for these white wings.

We sit down next to each other, though there's a big space between each seat. Drake looks comical perched on that tiny stool, chin in hand with a pinched brow.

"What are you thinking about?"

He shakes his head. "That it now makes sense why Sap likes you so much. She was drawn to you, though she likely didn't realise why. Same with the sea serpents—Aero told me about that encounter. They are both creatures of the world and your parents were born directly from it."

"Penis serpents," I correct, because he needs to know when he's incorrectly labelling something. Don't want the poor guy living his entire immortal life in total ignorance on the matter.

He smiles, leaning in to peck me on the nose. "Sorry. Penis serpents."

"Penis what?"

We spin around on our teeny stools.

Sol's approaching, silver wings out proud and fucking glorious—though he's looking a bit worse for wear, with dark circles shading his eyes and his hair all dishevelled. Looks like he forgot to shave this morning, too.

"Inside joke," Drake says, eliciting a huff from Sol.

Oh well, at least no heads are rolling. Yet.

Sol may look tired, but his wings are in fine fucking form.

Extra shiny, the feathers smooth and streamlined, like they've been recently preened ...

Yeah, my wings pop out with *that* thought, flapping in the wind all fluffy and flirty.

Sol wears a blank expression as he notes their little welcome dance. I roll my eyes, turning back to face the empty table. Traitorous twits, he obviously isn't interested in them right now. Do they not know how to hold a grudge or take a hint? Their lack of emotional maturity is becoming tedious.

Sol takes a seat opposite me and I roll my eyes for the second time in less than thirty seconds, choosing to focus on my hands clasped together in front of me, even though the sight of Sol coiled up on that tiny stool has me biting back a smile.

Drake stands, picks up his seat like it's a fucking pebble and plonks it down beside me. He then places his hand over mine, stroking my fingers with his thumb in smooth, comforting strokes.

"You two seem pretty cosy ..."

I flinch at the cutting tone of Sol's voice, feeling like I've done something wrong, even though Drake's assured me I haven't. I can't see this conversation ending well—not with tension tightening the space with only two Sun Gods present.

Aero flashes onto the seat next to Sol, his wings out, catching the mid-morning rays which highlight all the glorious undertones. He also looks as if he hasn't slept all night, though I still bite my lip, dragging my eyes over him with a long, leisurely stroke.

He may be in my sin bin, but my uterus can still appreciate a good meal.

My wings spread themselves wider, trying to gain his

fucking attention, succeeding only in fighting for space with Drake's overextended wings.

Aero smirks and Drake clears his throat, just as Kal lands on one of the two remaining seats, his black wings billowing about behind him.

He also looks a bit tired, though it doesn't detract from his sex appeal. My vagina does a little dance, hoping to lure him into her cave so my fertile womb can suck his penis dry.

Closing my eyes, I try to stem my rogue hormones. Full squad here and my wings are stretched to full fucking wingspan, because they're just as randy as my uterus now that all my Sun Gods are on one small island, on their tiny chairs, looking like four tasty snacks.

Goddammit, being in heat is hard work.

I'm surprised Aero hasn't mentioned anything yet, he's the only one privy to my non-stop internal vomit. He doesn't even seem pissed about everything that's happened since we last spoke …

The wind shifts—just slightly, though it's noticeable for anyone with a keen sense of, well … everything.

Aero sniffs the air with a furrowed brow. "What's that smell?" The wind shifts again, and his eyes fucking widen, gaze landing directly on *me.*

My face heats. "You didn't know?"

My Dawn God stands, and fucking explodes. Metaphorically. "No, I didn't fucking know! You've cut us all off! We've been in complete fucking silence; too afraid to make a move for fear we'd lose your trust forever!"

I stare at him, wide eyed and blinking. Well then … I guess they really do care about me.

"Are you in fucking *heat?*"

Shiiiiit.

I look around the table—noting Sol, Aero and Kal are surging with energy, their chests wide and heaving, wings poised behind them ready to propel my Gods forward should I expose my randy uterus. Perhaps if I ignore the 'heat' comment, it'll disappear altogether.

"What do you mean I 'cut you all off'?" I croak.

"Fuck this," Aero snaps, eyes darkening. He strides towards me, only to be stopped in his tracks by a growling Drake who looks poised for battle.

"Let me pass," Aero growls. "I need to fucking smell her."

"Easy, Dawn ... you've already shown you can't control yourself around her." They're up in each other's faces, like dogs threatening to scrap over a rotting carcass.

I put my face in my hands and groan.

"And you can? Why the fuck does *your* scent have traces of *hers* in it, Drake?"

Ahhhh fuck …

I look up to catch Aero's gaze flick from my neck to Drake's.

"You fucking *mated* with her? After everything you did to stop her from mating with *me* first? Un-fucking-believable!" Aero pushes forward, putting his forehead to Drake's and growling like a rabid beast, his wings flared to their full span. "Was she in heat when you fucked her? Did you put your fucking seed in her? You know she's not ready for that shit!"

My randy uterus thinks otherwise, but we're ignoring her.

"No, Dawn. I'm fairly certain I didn't impregnate her, even though she was fucking *begging* me to."

I groan again.

Holy fucking Sun Gods, this is *not* going according to plan.

They start bickering in a language I recognise, but don't understand. It's the same ancient tongue I spoke on the day I summoned them accidentally, when all I *really* wanted to do was jump off that goddamn cliff to escape this fucked up world. Now I'm standing here, wearing a chastity belt to protect my salacious uterus, trying to placate my four Sun God boyfriends into a consensual and feasible reverse harem situation while I'm in fucking heat. This is about as fucked up as it gets.

I frown, feeling a force pushing against my body … like it's trying to gain purchase, but it keeps slipping off. I shift my attention to Sol, who's watching me, as still as a fucking statue. Every muscle in his body is tensed, his canines long and lethal.

He clears his throat, then shifts his attention to the table in front of him.

Weird.

I thought he'd be the one arguing with Drake for mating with me. I'm glad he's not. Something tells me this island wouldn't last long if they were.

Kal stands, takes three steps towards me, and pauses. I know I should be scared of him, considering my lady bits are screaming to be doused in jizz, and Drake did say my vagina smells super good right now. But that's not the point. Kal's still *supposed* to be in my sin bin, but I just can't bring myself to move away. He *did* give me two days of blissful happy web, after all …

He opens his arms out wide. "Little Dove?"

Yeah, okay, only because that makes me want to cry. Fucking hormones. I tumble into his arms and my wings snuggle into my back, allowing his to wrap around me— thick black feathers caressing me in all the right places. I nuzzle into his chest, allowing my body to sink against his as he shelters me from the lashing wind. His wings are so much bigger than mine, and being wrapped in them? It feels like home …

Yeah, that's precisely what it is.

Home.

Kal sighs. "There she is ... fuck." He gestures to his heart, "It's been empty here, not being able to feel you." I sigh, nuzzling further into him while he takes a deep whiff of me. "Dell ... you *are* in fucking heat!"

I groan, my body pressing into him even as my mind *screams* at me to peel away. I barely notice his grasp tightening, but then he lets me go, wings uncurling while he steps back in stoic, stiff movements. His eyes are black and glazed over, muscles twitching and he's frothing at the mouth through clenched teeth; his canines long and lethal.

Wow, really glad I'm wearing that chastity belt right now, because I'm pretty sure he's frothing over the scent of my superb smelling vagina.

"Can you hold two?" Drake yells, and it takes me a moment to realise he's talking to Sol, who's standing on the table now, red faced, his brow dappled with sweat.

"I can barely hold Kal, he's fucking lost it."

What the hell's going on? Are Drake and Sol communicating like adults for once?

Drake's on the ground keeping Aero pinned, thrashing beneath him like a semi-contained beast.

Fucking hell.

I drag in a deep whiff of the air about me, scenting a plethora of male arousal. Pretty impressive considering the fierce wind gusting around us.

Honestly, I don't know what all the fuss is about, I smell normal to me. This is ridiculous. I knew babysitting these guys was going to be a challenge, but we've just reached an all-time low on that front.

I sigh and walk to the edge of the rock, then turn to face my unruly Sun Gods, ripping my dress to just above the waist as I do so, which catches all their fucking attention.

"I'm wearing a chastity belt, okay?" I signal in the general area of my uterus. "This is out of bounds. Yes, I'm in heat.

Yes, I mated with Drake. No, it wasn't while I was in heat. No, it doesn't mean I don't want to mate with the rest of you. I know I'm being greedy, and it may be exhausting, but fuck it—I think I'm qualified enough to handle the workload. Now, let's all sit down around that table on those teeny tiny stools and talk about this like adults, or else I'll go hang with the megalodons who may or may not like the taste of white fucking wings!" I'm panting, because hormones are hard work. But my Sun Gods have stopped scrapping and are looking at me like I actually made sense to them. Thank fuck.

Slowly, they make their way back to their seats, hissing occasionally and watching each other sideways. Still, I count this as progress.

I glance down at my chastity belt … I thought it would be the thing to *cause* the drama. Turns out, it did the exact opposite. Glancing at Drake, I give him a little smile. He nods, and that tether connecting us pulses with light.

Aww, I think we're strengthening our bond. Go us.

I walk towards my seat, but don't sit down. At least when I'm standing, I'm actually looking *down* at them on those little stools, and it makes me feel like I have the upper hand … sort of.

"Why can't you hear me anymore?" I ask Aero, who's pouting.

He shakes his head, running his hands over his face. "You cut off from me the moment you fucking sin-binned me. I haven't been able to hear or feel you at all. I could tell you were still alive, but my energy kept hitting a wall. Like you didn't *want* me."

Oops. Probably why none of them slept. I guess that means they really *do* care. I pan my vision around the table, each of them lacking colour and high on frustration, with taut jawlines and crumpled brows. Must've been pretty shitty seeing their girlfriend run off to mate while they sat in the sin bin thinking I didn't want them. Though I'm not sure how I cut them off in the first place.

"Am I broken? Why can't you reach me anymore?"

"I can now," Kal remarks.

"I never stopped being able to." Drake tosses in his token's worth, which causes the rest of them to hiss.

I throw him a 'don't go there' look.

"We know that, *fucker*," Aero snaps.

"Guys …"

"Not my fault you fucked up," Drake growls.

I sigh. Yeah, we fucking went there, didn't we?

"Do you want to take this to the air, dickhead?"

How did they survive all these years without a woman to keep them from killing each other? That's what I want to know.

"Want me to pulverise your insides, Dawn? I can tell you now, it won't fucking tickle!"

"Stop!"

I'm really surprised when they stop their bickering and actually listen. I look at Kal, slumped on his stool with his arms crossed. "Can't you just 'happy' them?"

He flicks his gaze to me and shakes his head. "Too much energy. It's better if they just get it out of their systems. That's what I'm trying to do." He's trembling, biceps wrapped in tightly clenched hands.

He can't happy net the others, because he's barely maintaining control over himself right now.

Massaging my temples, I wonder if it's possible to get an immortal fucking headache, because I'm pretty sure I'm getting one now. "Am I doing something wrong?" I ask Sol, even though he's on my shit list.

He shakes his head. "It's the opposite. You're learning to block us, which means you're strengthening the muscles required to use your own abilities one day."

I frown at him, even though he's the only one being *remotely* helpful right now. "But … I don't have any abilities."

"That's not the case, Dell. I was trying to compel the fuck out of you before and you only batted an eyelid. Could you feel it?"

"I could feel something. What were you trying to get me to do?"

"Doesn't matter now, you sorted it on your own." He shrugs, then turns his attention to the table top, features etched with concentration, closing off *yet again.*

Aero slumps further into his seat, sighing dramatically and capturing my attention. Must be hard for him, he's so used to being inside my head all the time, and to be fair, I was getting kind of used to having him there. My mind's a tangled web that will never be completely functional, but with Aero in there I feel like I'm not just speaking to myself anymore. The initial invasion of privacy now feels like a necessary part of my *soul.*

I don't want this space between us. Now that I've had time to consider, I understand what he did wasn't to hurt me —it was to help me gain back my own equilibrium. It was to—

Aero smiles, his face softening. "Thank fuck for that, I can hear you again. What did you do?"

I shrug, smiling. "Forgive you?"

He laughs, scratching his head. "I guess that makes sense. I'm sorry I fucked up."

"Sol fucked up, you were just trying to patch the wound." I look at Sol still staring at the table, and roll my eyes.

"Drake, you mentioned something about a 'prophecy' earlier then brushed it off. You thought I didn't notice but I forget nothing. What were you talking about?"

"Idiot." Sol shakes his head, growling. "I thought we discussed not to bring that up around her?"

"It just fucking slipped out!" Drake looks guilty, shrinking on his stool, massive shoulders curling forward.

"What did you mean by it?" I glance at the others, all looking pissed, then back at Drake. "Well?"

Drake clears his throat, shifting on his seat.

It's Sol, once again, who answers … albeit after a super dramatic sigh. "'Gleitz adorn, de mel te heist. Sevana ta lein'—translating to, 'The sun will rise and fall, the world will love them all.'"

"This is a bad idea," Aero mutters.

Sol blatantly ignores him.

"Those were the words that bound us to you on the cliff —the words that drew us to you. They speak of our connection with the world and the world's creatures; of the ebb and flow of energy between us. But they also have a deeper meaning."

Yeah, it's pretty fucking obvious.

I take a few deep breaths while I freak the fuck out. "So, the way I'm … attracted to you all, it's because of this *prophecy?* I never had a choice in the matter?"

Sol frowns. "Guess that's one way of putting it …"

"Is there another? That's seriously fucked up, like an arranged marriage except it's not at all, it's an arranged fucking harem!" Yeah, okay, I'm hyperventilating. This shit is heavy.

"It's okay, Little Dove …"

"No, it's fucking not!" I run my hands through my hair, fingers getting caught in all the tangles and adding to my frustration. "Wow, I thought I finally had control over my vagina … how wrong was I? This is like a kick straight to the labia!"

They wince. Yeah, that was probably a bit too graphic.

"Don't," Aero warns, looking directly at Drake.

"It's the only thing that's going to calm her down, arsehole," Drake growls, returning his attention to me. "Dell, you do have a choice."

This dick. "That's rich coming from the one I've mated to for life. You could have shed some light before you sunk your teeth into my fucking neck!"

"Okay, granted," he offers me a small smile, "but it really would've ruined the moment ..."

I can see his regret the moment he says it, slapping his palm to his forehead, but I jump on that comment like a God sucking leech because I'm a hormonal fucking mess right now. *"Ruined the moment?* Wow. Just wow. How's that for thinking with your penis?"

Yikes, I sound crazy. This is going to turn out to be a lesson on 'how to lose a Dusk God in twelve hours'.

Aero's smiling. "You're doing a shit job, mate."

"Fuck off, Dawn."

"Ugh!" I walk to the edge of the rock, from where I may or may not dive in and go swimming with the megalodons.

Okay, that's a bit dramatic, I really just need some space. But then Sol's all up in my face, blocking my way with his big fucking shoulders.

"There's a reason we didn't want to tell you. There are some things we didn't think you were ready to hear."

"I'm not ready for a lot of shit Sol, doesn't seem to stop any of you."

I move to push past the bastard, but he grabs me by the shoulders, halting me in place. I bare my canines, stand on my tiptoes, get right up in his face and hiss.

Nose to nose, he hisses back.

I don't move an inch. I refuse to back down to him.

He fucked up.

Not me.

My beast cracks her eye open. I'm pretty sure she's not

about to bite him on the neck, but I wouldn't put it past her to bite his cock clean off.

I wrestle the bitch back down, just to be safe. Let's not get too hasty here, I haven't completely set aside the idea of him prodding me with his rod in the future … if he ever learns how to apologise like a good little ten-thousand-year-oldish God.

"Drake wasn't lying," he growls.

Drake huffs, but I ignore him. He's one small step away from landing in my hormone-induced sin bin.

"You do have a choice. Dell … your *mother* had a choice."

Fuck.

I pull my lip back down over my canines. I never considered that my mother would be closely associated with my Sun Gods … rookie mistake right there. "Please, please tell me none of you boned my mother."

Sol frowns. "None of us 'boned' your mother, Dell. We did love her though—for the short time we knew her—like the sun loves the soil. She was gentle, pure of heart. She was everything good in this world." He clears his throat. "Your father was created at the dawn of time, as we were. Your mother, however, was not."

"What's that supposed to mean?"

He looks over my shoulder at the others, hesitating. "It means she was young … much, much younger than us. Edom, your father, asked the world for a worthy female, someone to provide him with a strong heir—and he got your mother, Mare. *Had* your mother, for a little under four hundred years."

I can *see* the shadows behind his eyes, dancing across his soul.

"We thought he killed her; we just had no proof until now."

Until me. Until he forced Aero to claw through my most painful memory.

I take a step back.

I want to ask about my parent's relationship—what changed between them and caused it to become so toxic. Why my mother felt it necessary to cut off her own daughter's wings to keep me from King Edom Sterling, her mate … and why he fucking *killed* her.

I don't ask, because part of my soul is screaming at me that I don't have the strength for it right now.

"So, you loved her …"

Sol nods, studying me intently. "Yes, but not in *that* way."

Right. "And my … seed donor? Did …" I clear my throat. "Did you love him?"

Sol shrugs. "There was a time, before he fell into the darkness, that we ruled together in peace."

"So, you loved him too?"

"Like a brother, yes. We always will, though the hate now overrides that significantly."

My mind jerks to the vision of the man with white wings and black eyes, slicing my mother's throat, panting through his bloodlust. I shake my head, banging my palm against my temple.

"Dell …" Aero warns.

"I'm fine," I growl, opening my eyes, dismissing that thought from my mind. Walling it up somewhere so I don't have to look at it.

I lift my chin, composing myself, ignoring Aero's penetrating glare which suggests he's expecting me to fall apart at any second. "So, I'm not bound by some stupid harem prophecy? Because it really does take all the lustre out of it if I don't have a choice in the matter."

Sol shakes his head. "You have a choice, now and forever. Nothing is forcing you to love us." He clears his throat and shuffles from one foot to the other, and folds his arms over his chest.

"Well … good." Catastrophe averted. I feel bad for yelling at Drake now, though that golden tether's holding strong, overlooking my crazy hormonal uterus like a champ. "Go sit down. I came here for a sex talk and we're going to have a fucking sex talk." I point to Sol's little stone stool, and to my surprise, he obliges.

I pan my vision around my four Sun Gods and draw a deep breath. This is going to be interesting. My vagina's urging me on, chanting for me to lock the bastards down and rein their godly penises in for her personal pleasure only … though I think it's important to remind the bitch that she's incredibly outnumbered and will probably have to share their cocks with my pucker, hand, and mouth if this is ever going to work. Logically thinking.

Aero closes his eyes and breathes through flared nostrils, fists clenching.

Oops. "Sorry, Aero …"

He draws a deep breath and opens his eyes, the remnants of darkness absorbing back into his pupils. "I'm fine."

He doesn't look like he's fine.

"Okay, so there's one of me, four of you. Drake said you're all okay with this idea, so I'm just going to jump right in and talk about it. How's this going to work?"

They look between each other, then back at me, their expressions really fucking blank. Except Aero, who still looks like he's in pain. I hope I haven't misjudged this entire situation … how awkward would that be?

"We've never shared one woman between all four of us, Dell. We're just as much in the dark as you are."

"Thank you, Kal, for clarifying that for me. You get a gold vagina star."

He smiles, straightens his shoulders and eyes off the others, looking very fucking pleased with himself.

"Okay, so who's shared before?" I deadpan, because I'm leading this congregation like a badass.

They do a group cringe.

"News flash, boys. I'm proposing a harem ... better get used to this shit." At least Aero no longer looks like he's battling an aneurism. However, he now looks like he's trying to fuse with his tiny stool.

"What's your problem?"

He shakes his head, clearing his throat while straightening. "Dell, we probably shouldn't talk about this in your ... state."

He's talking about my hormonal uterus, and that just makes me really fucking angry. Even my beast has cracked an eye open. I let her loose for a second, leaning our fists onto the table and eyeing the fucker off. "Do you really want to go there, Aero?"

He puts his hands up in submission, probably worried we'll chew his cock off. My beast is very fucking proud of herself when I rein the bitch back in.

"Sol and I have shared a number of times," he blurts out, really fucking quickly.

Maybe it's not so bad being in heat, after all? My men are so busy tiptoeing around my spurting hormones that I bet I can get almost anything out of them. "Number of times?"

He shrugs, mumbling something I can't hear.

"Pardon?"

He clears his throat and offers me a sheepish smile. "Few thousand, give or take."

I choke down my next breath.

Fucking Dawn and Day babies, that's a bit excessive. No wonder he was trying to become one with his seat.

I'm just standing here, staring at him, trying to absorb

that not-so-little piece of information. I add a few thousand to that number because he's probably underestimating significantly to save my hormonal shock.

I glance at Sol, who's smirking. He's obviously proud of his shared cock mileage.

Bastard.

Kal puts his hand up like the teacher's fucking pet. "While we're at it, Aero and I have shared before, too." He's trying to catch a piggy back ride on that tidal wave of God sex I just absorbed. "Nowhere near that much though," he hurries to add, grinning like he's just become my favourite.

"I see." Fucking hell, these Gods.

Seems Aero's quite the exhibitionist.

There's a flash and Aero's all up behind me, kissing down my neck, running a finger over the upper edge of my left wing, and taking complete advantage of my stunned fucking vigour. I groan, leaning my head back, exposing my neck to him.

He grabs at the waist strap of my chastity belt and tugs my arse back into his crotch. I gasp at the firmness of his cock pressing against me, teasing my fervent uterus who forces me to grind against him.

He laughs, running his canines along the skin of my neck. "Don't be so shocked, baby. Seems you rather enjoy it, too."

"Stop talking," I moan, fumbling for the key to my womb. "Fold me over the table and fuck me …"

My randy uterus made me say it.

He growls in my ear, sending tingles all the way to my toes.

I'm vaguely aware of Sol standing. "Dawn, I'm about to shift you back to your fucking seat, mate."

Aero laughs against my throat, giving my hips another firm tug. "Don't pretend like you're not enjoying the show,

Sol." He flashes back to his tiny stool, leaving me all hot and fucking heady.

Cheeks searing, heart racing, I clear my throat and drop the key back between my breasts, trying to compose myself as my uterus comes to terms with the fact that she's not about to be coated in Dawn jizz.

Aero smirks at the other three, paying particular attention to Drake as his eyes start their slow fade back to the safe, molten amber—proving he's got more sense of control than we all thought.

"Been practising?" Kal asks.

Aero shrugs. "I've had to get used to the fucker lately. So yeah, I guess you can say that."

Kal nods, looking impressed.

I scrunch up my nose, wishing I didn't tear half my dress off in a fit of dramatic rage. There's nothing to keep the scent of all my fertile juices at bay. Now that the tap's been turned on down there, even *I'm* turned on by the smell of myself.

Aero laughs and I huff out a sigh.

"So, no sex when I'm in heat, okay? Not yet, anyway. I'm probably a few decades away from the 'children' thing." I look at Drake, who's pouting. "Sorry ..."

He shrugs. "I've waited millennia to find a woman my beast approved of, I'm a patient man. At least Sap will be out of her teenage phase by then. I can't imagine those years are going to be easy."

Smiling, I throw him a wink. "Don't worry, I'll help you through it." Then I catch myself, realising I sound like a grade A God stalker. "As long as I haven't gotten sick of your penis and moved to the East, of course."

Drake blinks rapidly at me, and I ignore my urge to lick his chin dimple ... with my vagina.

I look at Sol and point to the contingency plan hanging between my boobs. "I've got this golden key now, so I won't be needing a piece of your floor anymore. Yay for you." I say that ... but it wouldn't be a bad idea to have a backup plan for my backup plan. It's good for a girl to feel like she can stand on her own two feet, especially if her harem of Sun Gods decides they're sick of her and her annoying wings. At least I've thrown him off my scent now. If a piece of his floor goes missing, he'll probably never suspect it was me.

Sol clears his throat, mumbling something in another language and making the rest of them roll their eyes. I frown. Wish I could talk arsehole. I feel a bit left out.

"Okay, good talk. Anything anyone would like to add? A 'team harem' chant or something? I'm all ears."

"Me," Kal cuts in, his voice sounding hard and serious.

"You have a chant? Quick work."

"No, but I do have something in my pocket I want to share with the table."

I really hope he's talking about his penis.

"Wait," I interject, and Kal pauses, hand wrapped around a piece of white parchment that's unfortunately not his penis. "How old is this table?"

Aero shrugs, "As old as us."

"And it's always had six tiny god chairs?"

They glance at each other, then group answer, "Yes."

I do the calculation in my head ... my mother, my four Sun Gods, and the King. Six chairs. Except my mother was only pulled from the world four-hundred fucking years ago.

"Whose chair is that one?" I ask, pointing to the charred one next to Kal's.

They stare at it, saying nothing.

"Hello? Anybody?"

Kal shakes his head, looking as pale as a fucking ghost and avoiding my eye contact altogether.

"Dell ..."

Finally.

I turn to Aero. "Yes?"

"You're right, that chair did not belong to your mother."

It doesn't take a genius to work that out, though it's nice to be validated. "Then who did it belong to? And why the hell is it charred black?"

He shakes his head, drawing a deep breath laden with emotion, "That's a story for another time. It's not an easy one to hear."

"Well that's a fucking cop out. What you really mean is that you don't think I'll cope." I fist my hands, trying to ease my urge to launch across the table and scratch his face in hormonal rage.

Drake strokes my wings, making them puff out dramatically. The tension in my body dissolves. "We're telling you it's hard to talk about, babe. Can you trust us on this, and trust that we'll tell you when the time's right?"

He strokes my wing again, and I slap him away. "Do you actually intend on telling me?"

He looks disappointed that I asked. "I do, Dell. When the time's right."

Bastard can't lie. He must be telling me the truth. "Fine. Keep your secrets. I can appreciate your limitations, unlike *some* people." I shoot a condescending glare at Sol, who conveniently avoids my eye contact, then gesture to the parchment in Kal's hand, "What's that?"

Kal's stature loosens, his face softening. "This is the reason I arrived late. A messenger delivered it as I was leaving."

He hands it to Sol who skims over it, curses really fucking colourfully, and passes it on.

"What is it?"

Drake frowns. "Suspicion. Has anyone seen you with your wings out? Aside from us?"

"I don't think so, I've been hibernating in your God

caves." I pause, before looking at Kal, eyebrows raised. "Cassian?"

"He wouldn't have said anything." Kal levels me with a predatory glare.

I guess that's the end of *that* line of thought.

"Actually," I say, digging deeper into my memory. "When you guys ripped away my happy web and let me free fall from the sky, I *did* see a flash of red feathers in the clouds. I thought I was imagining things …"

Sol growls, deep and guttural. "He has to be testing us, trying to weed out the rumour. He probably doesn't believe it himself, but he knows the prophecy and he's working it to his advantage." He slams his hand down on the table and I jolt. "With a warded fucking invite that we can't avoid."

They grunt, nod, mutter amongst themselves while I'm standing here getting really fucking salty. How *dare* they leave me and my hormonal uterus out of this conversation. I snatch the parchment from Drake's hand and dash to the water's edge, four Sun God's hot on my heels. I turn, throwing them all a steely gaze.

The parchment is beautiful, flecked with lemongrass. I give it a sniff, noting an odd metallic scent, before reading aloud the words elegantly scripted in black ink.

'You are hereby invited to dine with King Edom Sterling, keeper of balance and ruler of all, at seven clicks past mid sun. Dress to impress and attend in the company of your greatest female pleasure.'

I look at each of them, picturing my white wings spurting from my back at the most unfortunate moment, and causing each of my Sun Gods to get spit roasted in the worst possible way.

No. Not happening. "I can't go to dinner with the fucking King!"

Okay, I know that's a bit presumptuous of me, but they do seem to enjoy me and if this thing is warded, then I'm not sure I have a choice in the matter.

Sol clears his throat, glancing at the others then back at me. "You're not …"

"Huh?"

"First things first," Kal states, holding up his magic hands. "We need to get those gorgeous fucking wings in."

I sense a distraction but smile, mind emptying like a bucket with a very large hole in it. A really fucking fertile hole. I lean forward on the table, splayed wide like a delectable, feathery feast and, ignoring the group groans, close my eyes and settle in for the ride. "Work your magic, big boy!"

CHAPTER TEN

They delivered me to the kitchen in the Day Kingdom, asked Nex to prepare me a feast, then took off into the Bright in a real godly hurry. Apparently it's already six clicks past noon—time flies when you're having sex talks with Sun Gods and smoothing over immortal drama.

Nex is great—he even asked me where I'd like to sit, then had one of the helpers set up a table on an overhanging balcony for me so I could eat while watching dusk snatch the light from day; a brilliant performance best described as looking like someone vomited gold glitter all over the Day Kingdom.

Stunning.

What a bonus that my dinner seat also offers me a perfect view of Sol's main entertaining hall and balcony, directly below and to the right of my perch. Hard to miss my four Sun Gods down there, looking delicious in the metallic God gear I love so much.

From my vantage point I can see Aero's gaze darting around, shifting from one foot to the other like he's nervous.

Hmmm. What's going on?

Four gorgeous High Fae women wander onto the balcony, chatting and giggling like they fucking own the place, drinking pink champagne out of crystal flutes ...

What the twat?

Hackles rising, insides seething, I glare at them in their corseted gowns fitted to complement their bodies perfectly, showing *just* the right amount of skin to make them appear sexy without looking like whores. They arch their necks, pushing their breasts out, throwing sultry glances at my Gods—*my fucking Gods.*

"Bitches," I mutter. "I know what you're up to, trying to catch the attention of my oversized penises." I pick up a dinner plate, take careful aim ...

Kal flicks a knowing look over his shoulder at Aero, who nods and leaves.

He's probably going back inside to collect more women.

Bastard.

I get back to my dinner plate dilemma ... which one do I aim for? Fuck it, any one will do. I pull my arm back as Aero flashes right beside me and almost makes me shit myself.

"What the hell, Aero?" I drop the plate and it shatters, causing four gorgeous immortal women to look my way. "Nothing to see here," I mutter, giving myself a little tap down to make sure I didn't piss myself either. "That was *not* kind!"

He quirks a coy smile. "Sorry. I could hear your pondering and wanted to come and give that hormonal uterus of yours a wee pep talk ..."

I lift a brow. "Oh really?"

"Mhm. We've found a way around the warded invitation, and I don't want you to feel threatened."

"How so?" My voice cracks at the end, but I try to ignore that.

"We had to get creative. We can't have those gorgeous wings of yours popping out in front of the King, not when we're at our weakest and you're not yet ready to defend yourself."

He's missing the point entirely. Or … perhaps he's doing that purposefully? "How did you work your way around it, Aero?"

He clears his throat, looking a little awkward, making my curious nerve arch an eyebrow. "We, ah, worked out we could take a different *type* of 'favourite female pleasure' without going against the grain of the ward."

I gesture for him to *hurry the fuck up* and *spit it fucking out*. The bastard's pussyfooting around my question, probably hoping I back down. Surely he knows me better than that by now?

He sighs. "We're each taking our favourite blrrrjb." He mumbles the last word so quietly I can't fucking hear it.

"Say what now?"

He coughs, looks away. "Blrrrjb." Perspiration is beginning to build on his forehead.

"What the fucks a blrrrjb?"

He winces, drawing a deep breath. "Blowjob, Dell. Fucking blowjob, okay? But it's no big deal, they mean nothing to us now. They're just a means to keep you safe. We can't take you, so …"

Yeah, this time I *feel* the very moment I close off from him. It's like a gate shutting around my heart. I'm not sure how I missed it when I did it the first time, probably because I was so riled up. Now, however, my heads clear as fucking crystal—aside from my raging hormones, that is.

Aero frowns. "Did you just cut me off?"

I smile ever so sweetly, doing my best to repress my inner hormonal bitch who wants to slice his fucking testicles off. "Mhm. I'm practising. Am I doing well?"

He nods, scratching his head. "Yeah, can't hear a thing …"

"Go me! Now, run along—it's rude to leave your guests waiting. I've got pudding to eat; custard filled sponge roll with a *very* thick drizzle of clotted cream. Nex is a great cook. Isn't he?"

"Fucking Nex," Aero grunts. "He better not lure you onto his cock with his pudding, or I'll slash the fucker."

Wow. Someone's got double standards.

"Anyway, you took that a lot better than I thought. We won't be long, baby." He brushes a hand along my cheek and I repress the urge to swipe it away like a psycho bitch.

I wave at him. "Don't rush!" Did that sound condescending? I hope not.

The moment he flashes back to the balcony, I ask one of the helpers waiting at the door to fetch me a small pickaxe and some godly fucking alcohol, because there's no way I'm staying *here* tonight while my Sun Gods hang with their favourite blowjobs.

In fact, I'm picturing my new harem … four really fucking sexy High Fae who sure as hell won't hang out with their so-called favourite blowjobs without giving *me* the chance to prove my own blowjob expertise first. I don't always bite the bastards off.

A blonde lady with a sweet face and purple wings arrives, requested tool in one hand, bottle of bubbly in the other.

"Your pickaxe, milady," she says, quirking a brow and placing it on the table. She then pours bubbles into a sparkly flute, leaving the bottle on the table next to my axe. "Will there be anything else?"

"Yes, one more thing." I take a gulp of wine and give her my cheeriest smile. "I wonder, do you have anything really cute for me to wear?"

"Of course, milady. You're a guest of the Day God, you

can have whatever you like. Are you after anything in particular?"

I nod and do a twirl. "Something that hugs my above average arse."

Her gaze flicks to the pickaxe, then back to my face, likely internally questioning my sanity before slipping off to 'find me something suitable'.

I drain my glass then refill the fucker, already feeling the effects of the super sweet strawberry wine. Swaying to the beat of my own tune, pickaxe in hand, I narrow my gaze on a particularly pretty area of floor to chip away at with my new favourite 'tool'.

Bastards.

It could just be the wine goggles, but I look *hot.* I give myself another admiring once over then prance out of the room in my silver sequined number, catching the light from the Fae orbs scattered about the place, making me look like a glittery hormonal *star.*

When my little blonde helper saw the fist sized piece of floor I was carting around, she got me a sweet little handbag with a long strap so that it can hang over my shoulder. It's pretty fucking heavy. Even so, it's good to have my contingency plan on my person, until I find somewhere to stash it, of course.

Glancing in one of the large hall mirrors, I give the little bag holding my contingency plan a pat, then do an unsteady twirl to get a better view of my sparkly lady lump.

Ohh yeah … my arse looks damn fine.

I sashay down the hall, trying to remember how to get to the kitchen, clasping the bottle of leftover wine in my unsteady hand. The alcohol seems to have muddled my memory, but I figure if anyone knows how to have a good time in this kingdom, it'll be Nex. He looks young enough to know the beat of the place. If I could only find that fucking kitchen …

It crosses my mind that I *may* have lost all sense or reason, and I'm possibly being led by my hormonal uterus, but I dismiss the thought fairly quickly. It's killing my drunken vibe.

I stumble across an opulent doorway. Hearing Sol's booming voice behind it, I press my ear to the door; ignoring the two guards with massive grey wings stationed either side, watching me with cocked brows.

Must be the room they're entertaining their favourite blowjobs in, at least until they leave for dinner with daddy dearest.

Before the guards can react, I shove the door open, swaying into the room like I own the place, catching the attention of four tight faced Sun Gods … and four frowning blowjobs.

"Dell … what are you doing?" Sol asks, eyeing me up and down, his gaze coming to rest on the bottle dangling from my hand.

I hiccup.

"Are you *drunk?*"

I shrug. "Maybe. I'm going out. I'm not staying locked in your sparkly tower while the four of you hang out with your blowjobs." I gesture to said blowjobs, who look at me like I'm a terrible inconvenience to their fellatio business.

Sol looks like he's about to explode out of his God gear.

I roll my eyes, taking another swig of my wine, though I then realise the fucker might very well be empty. I turn it upside down, open my mouth, poke my tongue out, and shake the bottle.

Nothing.

Throwing the girls a wink, I circle the rim of the bottle with my tongue before lowering the bottle to peer down its neck, confirming the solemn fact that it is, indeed, empty.

"Damn," I slur, frowning. I put the bottle on a nearby table, then stumble over to a handsome man, clad in a faultless white suit, bearing a tray laden with numerous glasses of the bubbly sweet stuff. "Yummy," I say, running a finger down his lapel and snatching a glass off the tray. I feel something tug at my conscience but push it aside. Giving the man my biggest smile, I thank him for the wine and turn back to the others.

I might be a bit tipsy, but I know exactly what's going on here … Kal's trying to put me to sleep, the fucker.

I see them all share a look, but totally ignore it.

"Where are you going?" Aero growls, taking a tentative step towards me.

I take a gulp of my wine. "I don't know, somewhere. Might go find myself another harem. Sol said High Fae like to share and I'm kind of hooked on the idea now."

They give a group growl and I roll my fucking eyes, ignoring the tether that's 'tugging' at my heart. I avoid looking at Drake. Besides, his cock is well and truly handled for the night by Miss Long Legs who's hanging off him like a wayward pubic hair. A really pretty one.

Looking at the clock on the wall, I realise they probably have about thirty seconds until they have to flash off to dinner with daddy dearest.

"What if your wings come out?" Kal pleads, trying *again* to push on my conscience. I give him points for persistence.

I shrug. "I'll ask someone to stroke them for me, I guess."

Yeah, that probably wasn't the right thing to say. Stupid drunken word vomit.

They come towards me, all four of my Gods. I take a step

back. The blowjobs look super confused but, damn them, even with creased brows they're still gorgeous fucking blowjobs.

I dodge Drake's lunge, remarkably, because I can barely feel my feet.

He snarls. "You're in fucking heat, Dell!"

I put my finger to my lips, eyes wide. "Oops. Think I left my essential fashion accessory behind, too." I run my hands down my body, pretending to feel around. "Nope, definitely not there. Oh well." I turn for the door, flick him the bird and sashay/stumble out of the room, chugging back the rest of my glass then clanking it down on the hall table.

Feeling a deep pressure squeezing my body, I laugh, looking over my shoulder at Sol, who's standing in the hall, wide eyed and feral looking. If I wasn't so drunk, I'd probably be frightened. "Oh, cute—you're trying to compel me! Bye now," I wave. "Enjoy your blowjobs!"

I take about two steps down the hall before Sol yells, "Dell, I wish for—" and they flash off into the Bright.

Hmm.

Cheeky Sun God. Good thing the invitation ward kicked in, keeping them on time for their evening out. I breathe a sigh of relief, though my heart begins to ache. I rub the bastard. "Pull yourself together!"

The men standing by the door look at me like I'm mad.

"Sorry," I drawl. "I have an unruly womb."

They quirk their brows, all four of them. Wait, no … six. My chest pangs again and I wobble down the hall on my barely functioning legs. Fucking heart. It's probably hurting because Sol showed he actually *does* care, if he was willing to use his wish to make me stay behind …

I slap myself across the face because I'm forgetting what's important here—the fact that I'm not their favourite fucking blowjob. I ignore the part of my *actual* brain telling me I haven't even given them one yet. That doesn't do my persuasive uterus any favours at all.

CHAPTER ELEVEN

I eventually found the kitchen, and after a bit of coaxing, Nex agreed to take me the short distance into town. He asked if we could fly, told me it's faster, but I told him I can't fly sober let alone drunk. I have enough faculties to know I probably would have drawn some super undue attention to my feathery lady friends.

Anyways.

He brought me to this really awesome 'rave'. It's basically a bunch of drunk High Fae grinding up against each other to the beat of the talented band on the podium over there, pumping out electrifying music beneath the night sky. Our only roof is the low hanging strings of glowing Fae orbs criss-crossing the darkness.

The music is speaking to my fucking *soul* or something, and even with my heavy bag swinging at my side, banging at my hip constantly, I can't stop dancing. I don't even care that I'm by myself in the middle of a sweaty, feathery mosh pit … I'm having the best time of my fucked-up life! I'm swaying my hips, jumping up and down with my hands in the air, flinging my head from side to side … probably whipping some unsuspecting High Fae in the face with my hair.

I don't care.

I'm *alive*.

Nex is watching from the bar, like he's here to protect my virtue or something. It's cute, really, that he's under the impression I have any left to protect.

I keep waving to him, trying to encourage him to dance but he just shakes his head and pats the chair next to him, a vain attempt at getting me to sit down. Killjoy. I had high hopes for Nex being my wingman tonight, helping me hunt down my new harem.

All this perspiring has made me *parched*. Water, that's what I need.

Panting, sweating and trying to keep my balance, I manoeuvre through the crowd towards the bar and Nex, only I can't feel my feet anymore and I stumble, landing on my knees in the middle of the dance floor, falling face first into some strange man's crotch. "Oomph."

Firm hands grasp around my underarms, hoisting me up and out of 'penis territory,' thankfully, because that's not a very nice way to say 'hi'.

"Sorry," I mumble, giggling. I'm not sure if I'm looking at him straight. Am I looking at him straight? "I drank a whole bottle of wine and I've never actually drunk alcohol before. I used to be a whore on a leash, so if I'm to be entirely honest, I'm surprised I'm still conscious."

He lifts a brow, studying me really fucking closely. "Do you need some water, ma'am?"

"Yes, how did you know? My tongues even hanging out. See?" I point to my tongue, now dangling from the side of my mouth, noting that he's quite good looking. Not a bad start to my new harem … I wonder how big his wings are. My womb has high expectations, probably because my heart belongs to my Sun Gods ... who have super impressive wings.

Did I really just think that?

He takes my hand and leads me to the bar, creating a nice straight path for me to walk through without coming face to face with any more penises. I tell my hormonal uterus that's a good thing, even though she's just interested in measuring their cocks against my built-in 'Sun God Dick Scale' to make sure they'll be good breeding material. She's a picky hormonal hoe. Me? I'm just happy none of the women here are being raped or whipped for insubordination.

Seems Sol was right—things *are* different in the Sun Kingdoms. I smile at the thought then proceed to guzzle back an entire glass of water in one hit.

"What's the little smile for?"

I look up at the man I'm now going to label my 'Water God,' because he brought me water when I was close to death by dehydration. "Can I just say, I'm very thankful for the water." I'm pretty sure me speaking about my former Sun God harem will entirely ruin the mood we've got going on here.

He laughs. "You're easy to please."

"Yeah, I actually am. All I need is regular orgasms and I'm right as fucking rain. I'm also really good at blowjobs, apart from this one time I ..." yeah, probably not the best time to tell my Water God that I chewed a guy's dick off. "We won't go into that."

He pales, lifts a brow, clears his throat and readjusts his pants.

I look down. Hmm, guess that's where all the blood from his face went. Straight to his dick. Not quite Sun God impressive, but I reckon I could work with it ...

My uterus isn't so sure, and even my vagina's having

trouble getting revved up, though this guy seems kind enough …

Probably time to address the elephant in the room. "Look, I don't know if you've noticed or anything but I'm—"

"In heat?"

I tilt my head to the side, looking at him with wide eyes. "Yes, great observational skills."

He shrugs. "It's hard to miss. Most of the men here in smelling range have one eye on you."

"Really? I had no idea. Though it's hard to know these things when you're seeing double." I scrunch my eyes up, trying to focus on said 'room of guys', and fail miserably. Probably because I'm no longer seeing double—it's more like triple, or quads. "Surely there are plenty of women here in heat though?"

He shakes his head. "Usually they keep out of places like this during that time … unless they're out to mate."

Righty-fucking-oh.

I feel a tug on that golden heart tether, making my chest ache in response. I sigh, looking around for Nex. Where the hell is he? Maybe this was a bad idea. But my men are off having fun with their blowjobs. I reach down and pat my little bag, making sure it still contains my contingency plan.

"Hey." My Water God tucks his knuckle under my chin, tilting my face up. "Come and have a sit with me around the edge somewhere. We can have another drink?"

I think about it for a moment before nodding. Maybe that's what I need … another drink.

He gestures to a spare table a little out of the way, next to one of the main exits. I weave through the crowd, stumbling a few times and almost landing face first into the edge of a chair, though I manage to make it to the table without knocking out a canine. I take a seat and wait for my Water

God to join me with our drinks, using the time to rest my head on the sparkly table.

It's not until he makes his way back over, balancing both of our expensive looking cocktails that are bright fucking orange, that I realise I might be out of my depth here—because another drink might just have me passing the hell out. Even so, I smile and take a sip, because I don't want to seem ungrateful.

He watches me as I fiddle with my little wooden straw. "You know, you're a beautiful woman … but I suspect most of your beauty is on the inside." He throws me a wink. "What can I call you?"

It may make my skin crawl, but that gets the attention of my randy fucking uterus … she loves that shit. And to be honest, it's nice to feel her actually respond to someone *other* than my Sun Gods. It solidifies their statement that I do actually have a choice about who I mate with.

"Dell." I take another sip. "Yours?"

"Rogue." He takes a sip of his drink too, avoiding the little chode straw entirely.

I frown at my own straw—I should probably do the same. Don't want to come across suggestive or anything.

I don't realise I'm leaning into him until he chuckles, threading his arm around my waist. "You okay?"

"Mhm. Just sleepy … think I've had too much to drink."

He clears his throat. "You can stay at mine tonight."

"That sounds nice. Sleep sounds nice."

He shuffles me around a bit and threads his other arm under my knees, then hoists me up.

It feels like only a few seconds before the pulsing music fades and the intense lights disappear, replaced with peaceful darkness.

One minute I'm flopping in the arms of my Water God,

the next he's frozen solid and I'm being lifted from him by a pair of firm, confident hands.

"Get the fuck out of here!" Sol's voice.

Awww.

He sounds really fucking angry, but my wings are excited to see him and pop out faster than they *ever* have before. They curl around us both, fluffing themselves up and making Sol groan a little. I smile into his chest, hear a few muffled gasps, then a flash of white light lands us in Sol's sparkly bedroom.

He's growling and holding me so damn tightly I'm worried I might actually *break*.

"Ouch …" I croak.

There's another flash of light followed by a relieved sigh or three.

"Where the hell was she? We searched the entire rave with Nex and couldn't see her anywhere!"

"Passed out in the arms of some dick."

I crack an eye open and see five concerned Aero's, five brooding Kal's and five fucked off Drakes. I rub at my aching heart … oops.

"How long have her fucking wings been out for?" Drake snaps.

"They popped out when I grabbed her, I had to rush her here before too many people saw. At least five did, but the fuckwit carrying her had already been compelled to turn around, so he missed the show." He lays me down on the bed, stomach first, pulling a cover over me really fucking tenderly; curling his hands beneath my drowsy wings and lifting them so he can tuck the blanket nice and high. They do a sleepy little fluff dance to show their appreciation at having his hands all over them.

Sol peels the bag off my shoulder. I try to battle him for it, but all I achieve is flopping an arm about uselessly. He takes a peek inside the satchel and smirks, shaking his head, before closing it up and setting it on the nightstand. I try to hide my burning face with a wing.

"Aero, go into my head and get his image. I need you to find him and see what his intentions were so we can deal with him accordingly. Someone carrying a girl who's almost unconscious out of a rave is *not* ok by me, whether it's Dell or not. If his intentions were bad, he'll be put to fucking trial."

I groan, because he sounds so feral and serious. "He told me I was beautiful!"

They roll their eyes at me, Drake hissing like a penis serpent.

"Oh, hush. You guys had your beautiful blowjobs with you."

"That was to fucking save you, Dell!" Drake throws his hands up as that golden tether goes a little taught. I put my hand over my heart in a pathetic attempt to hold it there. "Fucking hormones. If I'm not plugging a baby up there anytime soon, maybe we need to assign her to Kal's harem when she's in heat next time. Isn't that what women usually do to keep themselves safe? Have little 'fertile sleepovers' where they all moan and bitch about their overactive hormones, and don't re-emerge for thirty-six hours until they're all back to fucking normal?"

I should probably be offended by that comment, but it actually sounds fun. I smile into my pillow. "Sign me up, I recently learnt the majority of them prefer females. They'd probably give me wingasms and take really good care of me."

They all groan, and Kal's eyes begin their slow fade to black.

Was it something I said?

Aero puts a hand on Sol's head, eyes glazing. Sol barely flinches as Aero takes the vision. It doesn't take long before

Aero's eyes snap back to the now and he removes his hand. "I've seen this guy before, he's on the Kings fucking *guard* ..."

Now they're all yelling in that foreign language I don't understand. I'd probably be pissing my panties if I wasn't so intoxicated.

I yawn wildly, hauling a huge gulp of air into my lungs. "I'm going to sleep. Take your argument outside." I give them a 'shooing' motion with my hand, before it flops back to the bed uselessly.

Sol mumbles something that sounds suspiciously like 'enjoy it while it lasts'.

"I'm not fucking leaving her," Drake growls. "We'll take turns watching over her tonight. Go find the fucker—bring him here if you need me to make him hurt."

"Psychopath," I mumble, nestling into the pillow and trying to ignore the fact that the entire world is spinning.

"I'm *your* psychopath, Dell. *Yours.* Don't ever fucking forget it again."

CHAPTER TWELVE

I wake, tongue stuck to the roof of my mouth, a dull headache sitting heavy behind my eyes. I crack my left eye open and wince from the sun banking through the window, illuminating Sol lying next to me on his back, shirtless, his left arm pillowing his head. He's all coiled muscle enveloped in a deep, golden tan. His powder blue eyes stare up at the ceiling like he's trying to learn its secrets, his face all hard lines and caged emotion. He swallows and his Adam's apple rolls beneath his skin.

I close my eyes, hoping he didn't notice I'm awake. I'm also hoping he does a classic Sol and pushes last night's antics under the rug, because I'm more than certain I'm going to be dished some serious words from at least three other Sun Gods once I recover from my self-induced hangover.

"Do you have anything to say for yourself?"

Fuuuuck.

I open my eyes. "Do you?"

He turns his head, looking me straight in the eye and fucking paralysing me. "I'm sorry I took away your liberties.

I'll—" he clears his throat, then draws a sharp breath. "You deserve better than that and I'll never forgive myself for what I did. I will spend the rest of my immortal life making it up to you."

Well, shit. He sounds so damn sincere that he almost makes me cry.

I was not expecting that.

Moments drip by and his words settle over me, easing at the open wounds on my heart—serrated flesh that suddenly doesn't feel so raw. It's not like Sol to apologise, let alone apologise so fucking earnestly.

He really does mean it.

"You *hurt* me. Don't do it again."

"I won't." He articulates each word, almost like a vow …

I feel the moment my heart forgives him, the gate lifting, and I watch as he breaths a deep sigh of relief, though his body still looks coiled like a sexy spring.

"Thank you," I finally whisper.

He nods, then looks back up at the ceiling. "Do you have anything to say for yourself, Dell?"

Dammit.

My wings tuck themselves tightly to my back … even they're embarrassed. Strangely, my uterus isn't all emotional and crazy this morning, leading me astray down the loopy hormonal tube. It's nice to feel myself again, even if I *am* saddled with a heavy hangover that I'm pretty sure I'll be suffering from for the next few days. "Um … I'm never drinking again. *Ever.*"

His jaw ticks and his biceps tense, his hand balling into a tight fist.

"I fucked up," I blurt.

"I want to punish you for it." He pushes the words through his teeth.

"What did you just say?"

"I said," he looks at me, his gaze steady. "I want to punish you for it."

"What do you mean?" Fucking vagina's frothing at the bit … she knows exactly what he means.

"I want to show you how last night made me feel."

My wings aren't sure what to do with themselves, tuck up or spread as wide as they can go? They're doing a bit of both because they're so indecisive.

I nod, eyebrows peaked, bottom lip caught between my teeth.

He exhales and pushes himself off the bed. Before I have a chance to second guess my decision, he's yanking on my hips so I'm sitting on my knees, but my chest and face are still pressed against the bed, the soft linen sheets consuming me. My skin pebbles with anticipation.

He tilts me to the side and rips the strap off my dress, allowing the front to flutter down. Our eyes meet, his tongue roaming over the tip of his canine, before his gaze lowers to the swell of my breasts. His throat bobs, a thick growl rumbling from his chest. He brings my hands together beneath me and coils the strap around my wrists, binding them to each other.

"Your safe word is 'white'. Do you understand?"

Ironic that he'd make my safe word the one colour that'll likely end up destroying us all.

The colour I'm saddled with.

I nod.

He runs his hand up one leg and then the other, calloused palms brushing against my skin, shifting my dress up and over my bum and exposing me to him wholly … fuck me, I forgot to wear underwear last night.

Oh no.

Sol snarls, the sound tearing through the room and

making my skin pebble as my wings try to tuck further into my back. "You went out without fucking *underwear*?"

Maybe I was better off without a uterus, because I have *no* idea how to manage this one. "It … appears that way," I confess, teeth snagging at my lower lip.

I'm not sure this is such a great idea anymore … but my vagina's already committed, and I don't *really* want to break her damp little heart.

He breathes heavily through his nose, pausing, hands clasping an arsecheek each. "I don't know what I'm going to do with you, Dell. You just don't fucking listen to me."

"I do listen, I'm just not very good at following instructions the vast majority of the time." Probably shouldn't have said that right now …

His chest rumbles and he pulls a hand off my right arsecheek, then flicks at my bud.

I almost jolt off the fucking bed.

"Stay still," he growls.

Holy fucking Day babies.

"Okay …" I do my best to still my hips—really hard when my vagina's purring.

He flicks at my bud again, harder this time, and though it stings a bit, I moan like a fucking beast because it's the perfect mix of pain and pleasure.

"Again …" I plead, arching to expose myself to him further.

"What do you say?"

"Please …"

He flicks again and it's a real bite. My arousal dribbles down my leg. Another flick and I almost buck straight off the bed for the second time.

"Stay still, Dell. Move again and I'll tie your fucking feet to the bed. Do you understand?"

"Mhm." I smile into the pillow, not sure if that convinces me to stay still or not …

He rubs at my throbbing apex, right on that bud he's just shown such biting, tender attention to—soothing me, smearing my juices through my folds, then upwards, to my taut little star, circling it with his finger and wetting the entrance. He parts my lips and slides two fingers into my lady love, at the same time probing my pucker with his thumb that's slick with my arousal. My body tightens reflexively.

"Relax," he orders, and I groan, enjoying the way he's filling me, though it's certainly not gentle.

It's smooth.

It's firm.

It's possessive.

He works his fingers in a circular motion, adding another finger and making me scream in frustrated pleasure-filled agony. I push against his fingers, grinding into him, but my body won't seem to slip over that orgasmic edge.

Sweat is beading down my temples, a slick sound filling the room as he works me over and over, my knees trembling in unrequited frustration, my muscles losing their ability to function properly.

I groan into the pillow, sinking my teeth into the linen, tearing holes that ooze miniature white feathers. Even my wings are rubbing themselves against Sol to gather some added friction, trying to gain that extra nudge I need …

"What's happening?" I gasp.

"How does it feel?" He growls. "How does it feel to lose control, Dell? To be completely at *my* fucking mercy."

Oh my Sun God, he's compelling my body, preventing it from spiralling into a pit of orgasmic pleasure!

I throw my head to the side, huffing feathers across the

bed as his fingers continue to swirl. "Isn't this … a waste … of energy?"

He brings his other hand to my bud, pinching it delicately between his fingers.

Holy.

Fucking.

Hell.

"Sol!"

"You're right there, aren't you? How does it feel to have something you want *right there*, while your body disobeys you entirely?"

This man.

I tug at my restraints, desperate to pin him to the bed with my teeth while I demand he give me my fucking orgasm … but he's really good at tying restraints, so it would seem. "This isn't fair!" Feathers are glued to my sweat soaked body, I'm heaving through the pleasure like a fucking animal, but he doesn't stop.

He just keeps.

On.

Going.

His thumb dips further into my arse and I scream at the bastard taunting me with his sinful fingers. "Just let me … fucking … have it!"

Sol's wings unfurl and he slaps me across the arse, not hard enough to hurt, but hard enough to tell me I'm being a naughty girl.

I push onto him harder, *hungrier* for that yearning orgasm.

"You'll get it when I let you have it."

I groan, needing more—needing to feel *him* inside me. "Just fuck me, Sol!"

His hand runs down my spine, bunching my dress around

my breasts, landing between my shoulder blades and pushing me further into the bed. "Do you want me?"

I nod into the pillow. "Yes …" I plead. "I fucking want you …"

His hand pulls away, fingers receding. I hear the shuffle of material before a large, hard, warm object is rubbing along my clit, through my folds. It occurs to me that I'm going to have to get used to that size really fucking quickly, because I'm pretty certain he's not going to go slow …

He slaps it against my clit, causing my body to spasm in anticipation. "You want this?"

I nod into the pillow. "Yes …"

He presses his dick at my entrance, swirling it across the most sensitive parts of me, almost pushing into me … then pulls away entirely, leaving nothing but a cool breeze as he blows a breath over my aching lady bits. "Do you know how *infuriating* it was, knowing you were out there, possibly fucking someone else, and knowing there wasn't a *thing* I could do about it?" He blows on me again, then presses his lips against my entrance and swipes his tongue through my folds, over my aching bud … *inside me.*

I whimper, trying to ride his tongue, but he pulls away before I get a chance to gather much friction. "I'm sorry …"

He hisses at me, "Say it louder."

"I'm sorry!" I scream, grinding my hips to gain back some of that lost friction.

He wraps his hands around my waist, pulling me back, positioning himself at my entrance. "This won't be gentle, Dell …"

"I don't *want* gentle!"

He ploughs himself into me, filling me so swiftly that I scream, but it's not in pain … it's in *delight*—my core rolling with the beating pulse of his cock. His body slaps against mine, over and over again as he fucks me. Hard.

I'm shifting forward with every thundering thrust, sinking my teeth back into the pillow as he rides me on the edge of this cataclysmic orgasm that just … won't … give. "Let me have it!"

He only fucks me harder, rides me harder, inserts a wet thumb into my arse—plunging deeply, causing me to moan in total fucking earnest.

"No," he growls. "Not until you give me your submission."

He shifts my knees, pushing them further out, tilting our position so the galloping slap of his body against mine is aggravating my clit with delightful tension …

It's fucking torture. He's torturing me with his delicious sex.

"Nobody else will ever understand you the way we do, Adeline. The way *I* do."

He just used my full name and I really don't give a shit. All I can think about is this man fucking me, this man I care for in ways I never thought possible, considering my internal disarray …

He's made some mistakes, yes.

So have I.

He's hard, he's rough, and he's really fucking abrasive … but I love him.

I look over my shoulder, watching him piston in and out of me, enjoying the way the sweat beads over those coiled muscles. "I know, Sol …"

His gaze darts to mine, wide and unblinking, wings going taut. "Good."

Then I'm screaming, falling headfirst into the most labia breaking orgasm of my entire fucking life. My whole channel is pulsing around his cock in wave after wave of pleasure as he continues to plunge into my aching, throbbing wetness. My wings sink into my back like the biggest sigh of relief.

He retreats, leaving me hollow and yearning, then flips

me over and sheathes himself inside me again, kneading the last of the orgasm from my body in delightful, rolling waves before he starts to build another.

Tugging my still bound hands over my head and holding them in place, he looks at me in a way he never has before … and I recognise it, because he's mirroring my emotions entirely.

No walls.

Exposed.

Bare.

He may not be able to say it to me yet, maybe never … but he loves me.

Sol *loves* me.

He nods, growling from his chest, as if he's reading my thoughts through the look in my eyes.

Looking up at this man, seeing the power he has over me as he rides me like the fucking God he is—watching those thick, powerful muscles tense and roll with every thrusting movement—seeing the sincerity in his gaze, the vulnerability … I realise I want him forever.

I want this man to be mine *forever*.

"Bite me …" I plead, and his eyes fucking widen. "Now!" I hiss and he fucks me harder, faster, eyes turning black.

I fucking love it. I fucking *bathe* in it. Because I did that.

I fucking did that.

I made him lose control.

"We can't take it back," he pants, his gaze dipping to my neck, the tendons on his own neck pulsing, thick and fast.

"Fucking … *bite* … me!"

Roaring, he lurches forward, sinking his canines so deeply into my flesh that I orgasm again, joining his own release, riding the pulsing spill of his cock as it empties deep inside me.

He groans around my neck, lapping at the small flow of blood spilling from the two wounds he's created.

I'm fucking salivating.

He pulls his mouth from my neck, eyes still wholly black, watching me with a furrowed brow.

"Release my hands," I order.

That brow creases further …

I snarl, my beast pouncing. We put the bonds to our teeth and tear through the fuckers ourselves before lurching forward and pushing him backwards onto the bed, his shimmering, silver wings splayed. We straddle him, running our hands along his chest and up the side of his neck, then force his head to the side, exposing his pulse to us.

Licking our lips, we pause, listening to his heavy pant; watching this powerful, controlling man laid bare to us, submitting himself to the throes of my inner beast.

We lunge.

Sol groans as we sink our teeth into his neck, licking at the blood that dribbles free and swallowing it back, revelling in the taste, then the feel of a silver tether snapping onto our heart.

I shackle my beast and moan into his neck, relishing the feel of his own tender rumblings beneath me.

I pull my teeth from his flesh and he pushes me off, climbs atop and pins me with his hips, towering above me, panting … devouring me with a carnal gaze that makes my satiated vagina wet with want. He smiles at me, takes my face in his hands, and kisses me so fucking firmly his teeth drag along my lip, drawing blood.

He pulls back so we're forehead to forehead, sharing fevered breaths; his wings folded around us, creating a cocoon. "Don't fucking scare me like that again."

I gulp, feeling the press of his erection between my legs, right at the doors to my vagina who's still recovering, but at the same time, aching to caress his throbbing manhood again. "I won't."

He thrusts his length inside me and I gasp, devouring it fully. Rolling his hips, he pushes deeper with every striking thrust.

Holy Day babies.

I'm collecting Sun Gods like tokens.

The kingdom's glistening with late morning light, emulating the shimmering ocean in the distance. I lean forward, pressing my body against the railing, drawing crisp air into my lungs.

Warm, calloused hands curl around my chest and stomach, tugging me back and locking me in place. I exhale, nuzzling into the man engulfing me. "I was just getting a good look."

"And I'm just making sure your feet stay firmly on the balcony." Sol dips his face to the top of my head, drawing a breath and exhaling a wash of warmth through my hair.

"I'm not the same person I was back then, Sol. That's not me."

His body becomes taut and moments drag by drenched in agonising tension. When he finally speaks, his words are clipped. "You still did it."

I turn around to face him, but he's staring at the horizon, a distant gleam in his eyes.

"Sol?"

"Dell."

Goddammit.

"I was sick of seeing the world suffer, alright? Seeing my world suffer while I stood on the sideline feeling useless. At the time, it seemed like the right decision."

His jaw clenches. "Do you regret it?"

"Yes," I say honestly. "You saw the worst in me that day … the part of me that's been worn to the nub from spending a lifetime trying to make up for my own shortcomings. I will regret jumping off that cliff for the rest of my life."

"Good."

I huff out a humourless laugh. "You're a hard bastard, aren't you?"

He looks me in the eyes. "I've lost sleep over it. We all have. We watched you throw yourself off that cliff and it was the most haunting thing I've ever seen in my very long life … because you were *happy* about it. You fucking *smiled*, Dell."

I stumble back a step, but his arms catch me. "Sol …"

"No." He rubs his hand over his face, exposing just how tired he is. The poor man probably hasn't slept in days. "I'm not good at this shit, okay? Just … let me get it out."

He looks towards the ocean again. He's uncomfortable, I get that. It's something I understand very fucking well.

"One day, when we bring children into this world … I want to know that they're not being born into a world where the better alternative to *living*, is for Fae to jump off a cliff to end their suffering."

"I …" Well, fuck. I don't know what to say to that. I end up saying the only thing I *can* say.

The truth.

"I agree."

His hold on me relaxes and he walks me back a step, pressing me against the low ledge and recapturing my gaze. Wedged between some shiny rock and a hard place, I have nowhere to go.

He picks me up by my thighs, spreading them wide and sits my arse on the balcony ledge. Nestling himself between my legs, he threads his hands around my back, holding me in place.

The cool morning air brushes over my bare skin—my long, tangled hair floating around us on the breeze. But I'm not thinking about the breeze … I'm thinking about that erection standing to attention between us. It seems an odd place to put an erection when I'm perched on the edge of a fucking ledge, one misguided thrust away from plummeting to my doom. I may have wanted it all to end back then, but now I know how much I have to *live* for.

"What are you doing?" I ask, eyes drifting upwards, taking in every curve and bulge of the naked man standing in front of me.

He leans forward, wings splayed, and tugs my bottom lip between his teeth, drawing a line of blissful pain that he proceeds to lick better with his tongue; permeating my senses with the coppery tang of blood. "Creating a new memory on a fucking ledge."

He reaches between us, fists his cock and begins to roll it over my swollen clit.

Yup. He's going to sex me right here, where I'm one slippery arsecheek away from sliding to my doom. I know the man has wings, and he can tear through that shimmering bright place if he wants to rescue me … but what if he miscalculates my trajectory and I end up skewered on a building? I feel like this hasn't been very well thought through. But right now, perched on a ledge and entirely at his mercy … I'm in no position to argue.

"I'm going to fuck you slowly, and with purpose." His voice is gravel close to my ear, my skin pebbling in response.

My body arches, muscles going taut as he teases me with slick, circular motions. It's agonizing, exhilarating torture …

His eyes drag up my body in a thick, languid stroke, coming to settle on my face and painting me with a hungry gaze. A rumbling growl rolls from his chest as his canines lengthen. He swirls his cock around my entrance, my body becoming clay to his touch. I throw my head back and moan to the sky.

"Look down, Dell."

I shake my head, unable to face the overwhelming intimacy of this moment.

"Now." He growls, and my eyes snap open at his tone. The hand that was guiding his cock wraps around the side of my face and he curls his body forward …

He's so close to nudging his way in. One small movement. One shift of his hips and he'd be inside me …

"I want you to watch me enter you."

Fuck.

"You're being kinky this morning," I jest, my mind's knee-jerk response to my emotionally-anal Day God being far from emotionally-fucking-anal.

He quirks a half smile that lights up his face entirely. "Get used to it. Watch." He grabs my chin and tilts my head, so I have a full view of his cock pressing at my wet entrance, the scent of my arousal infusing the space between us. He shifts his hips and slowly sinks himself into me, inch by glorious, devastating inch, my thighs trembling from their place wrapped tightly around his hips.

"Holy fuck …" I gasp, shifting my body, trying to readjust to his size filling me.

He drops his lips to my forehead and starts to move, pistons in and out of me, muscles rolling with the force, his core battling to keep me perched on the ledge.

I've never relied on anyone, much less willingly put my life in someone else's hands. It's too much for my little whore heart to handle, my hands coming to grip around his biceps as I struggle to hold on to my fraying composure.

My body may want this, but my mind's sinking … fast.

"Sol … I think I need a moment."

"No," he growls. "You're going to watch my cock slide in

and out of you while I fuck you on this ledge, then you're going to fall apart in my arms knowing I'll never let you fall."

I open my mouth to speak but he captures it with his own, silencing me with his lips and probing tongue, tasting my hesitation while I feed on his persistence. My frustration airs itself in a strangled moan and he ends the kiss, muzzling my frenzied thoughts with the jerking of his hips; filling me with pleasure, draining me of my doubts with each delicious thrust, while my life hangs in his hands.

When I finally succumb—my back arching further off the edge, my toes curling in ecstasy, and my core pulsing around his cock as I milk him of every last drop—it's not just my body that breaks for this man as he hungers over my breast, cradling me while we teeter on the edge of the unknown …

It's my soul.

My heart.

My everything.

"Where are the others?"

Sol's laying on top of me, his feathers catching the morning light shafting through the open balcony door. I'm surprised I can breathe; he's so fucking heavy, but I'm strangely enjoying the pressure of his body holding down my own, especially after what we did out there on the balcony, then continued in here …

It's like he's anchoring me in place.

The old Dell would've been running for the hills by now. The *Eastern* hills.

He clears his throat, lifting his head and threading his hands beneath his chin, over the upper rounds of my breasts so we're sharing breath. "Sleeping. We were up all night."

"Sleeping … locally? Do their rooms have balconies overlooking ours? I have so many questions right now …"

He quirks the faintest smile ever. "I have plenty of spare rooms, Dell. They didn't want to leave, so I placed them far enough away that they wouldn't be distracted or woken up by you screaming out my name during the last two rounds."

I blush and look away. He knew what was going to happen the moment he climbed into bed with me earlier. "I wasn't screaming *that* loud."

He grabs my chin and shifts it firmly, so I have no choice but to look at the bastard. "You were, and I fucking loved it." He steals a kiss, swift but lethal, draining me of the ability to think straight before he pulls back, wings disappearing, and rolls off me onto his back.

I miss the weight of him but at the same time, I'm really fucking gooey and I smell like I've just spent a day in the throes of whoring, except I haven't … I've been mating with my Day God.

He closes his eyes, tucking his left hand under his head and making me want to bite that bicep that's bulging so deliciously.

"I'm going to take a bath before I crust over," I whisper, getting no response except Sol's deep, heavy breathing. I kiss his jawline, can almost taste his deep, salty scent. His white hair, cropped short at the sides, falls over his face, masking his left eye. Full, plump lips are almost pouting in his sleep.

He would hate to hear me say it, but hell, this man is pretty.

I crawl off the bed and tiptoe through to the washroom, closing the heavy door with a soft thud, hoping the sound didn't wake my slumbering Day God. He needs his sleep after all those gold vagina stars he just received.

I parade my naked body across the excessive bathroom floor, ignoring the many strategically placed mirrors. Kinky Sun God, I bet he has fun with those ...

The constantly steaming bath in the corner extends outside, allowing for both indoor and outdoor bathing options, offering a delightful view of the city below and the ocean beyond. I step into its warmth, sinking low and relishing the feel of the water against my skin; soothing places I hadn't realised needed the attention. Steam rises around me and the constant, heavy trickle of water sends little waves over the water's surface, lapping at my nipples.

The trickling water, the steam, the heavy warmth lulls me. Dancing my fingertips over the surface, my mind starts to wander …

This time last night, I could never have imagined Sol and I would get to this point. His silver tether tugs at my heart with the thought and I smile. My thoughts shift to Drake, and our golden link does the same.

How quickly things can change.

I'm done with disappointing them. Letting them down. Perhaps I need to set my sights on a goal, something my Sun Gods would be proud of.

Something my mum would be proud of …

Wading outside, the cool air caresses me. Sun kissing my skin, I close my eyes and dip beneath the surface, feel the webbed tangle of my hair floating around me, rejoicing in the sensation of weightlessness as the water soothes away the remnants of the last two glorious hours. But not the memory … never the memory.

I sense a shadow blocking the sun. A cloud? No … it's a clear day. I open my eyes to a watery haze and feel something wrap around my neck.

I struggle, kicking out, wedging my fingers under what I realise is a thick fucking rope, bubbles pouring from my mouth as the shadow engulfs me.

Something hard and heavy collides with my temple and knocks me out cold.

CHAPTER THIRTEEN

I come to nursing a headache in a dark room, cold air nipping at my naked body, peaking my nipples and making me shiver.

Gods-fucking-damnit.

There's nothing except darkness and the scratching, jittery sound of cockroaches scuttling about. Actually, they sound bigger than cockroaches ...

I'm hanging by my hands, mouth bound, back pressed against a cold wall slick with mildew. My pointed toes kiss the ground, barely keeping the pressure off my aching wrists. There's an overwhelming stench about the room, a conglomeration of piss, vomit, and shit. Pain, suffering, rape ... and death.

Unfortunately for me, this is not looking good.

I try to scream but it comes out as a muffled whimper, because of the ball of material stuffed in my mouth, challenging my gag reflex.

Typical. I've gone from sexing my Day God into blissful oblivion to this bullshit. He's probably furious right now, thinking I pulled some sort of rash stunt again. I look internally for that silver tether, breathing a dramatic sigh of relief when I find it tucked away safe and sound, right next to my golden one.

My men are safe… well, at least two of them are.

Something prods my arm—gently at first, before applying more pressure, as though testing. I freeze, try to calm my breathing, my erratically beating heart. Whatever it is feels hairy and by no means small. If I ever wanted a prodding probe to be small, tiny even, it would be now.

It must decide this new, undiscovered territory is worth a visit because the next thing I know, it's scuttling up my arm. And yes, it's large. Very fucking large. It's probably a bird eating spider that's developed a taste for Fae.

Sinking my teeth into the material gag, I try not to move … difficult when you're hanging by your wrists and teetering on your aching toes.

A lock slides open with a heavy grind and the large, hairy thing freezes, though that's not necessarily a good thing—the fucker was almost off.

Another lock clanks open, and there's the sound of a chain smacking the door as it falls … they seriously overestimate me. It's not until the *third* lock clicks that I finally hear a handle turn. The door is pushed inwards and the room floods with lantern light, causing me to squint away from the assaulting brightness. The smell of cheap tequila and decaying cunt fills my nostrils.

"Is that her?" The sound of footsteps draws near.

I blink furiously, my eyes slowly starting to adjust to the light. Finally able to focus, I take in the image of the man—the monster—standing before me.

I suck in a shuddering breath.

Fuck.

I'm fucked.

Heavy, black bags pool beneath his eyes. Stubble, thick

and uneven, clings to a sallow, tight complexion. Eyes black as the night, hair red—as if it's been dragged through a puddle of blood.

"That's her. Get the others," says the cock from Kroe's— the red winged legionnaire who put a feather up my twat after beating me senseless a few years back.

The one Aero tortured.

I hope fuckery isn't on the menu, though, by the look in his eyes, I'd say that's exactly what's on the fucking menu.

My eyes dart hopelessly around the room, looking for anything I can use to gain an advantage. But the room is empty apart from a small fireplace set into the far wall, thick logs stacked beside it and a basket of kindling. Something tells me that fire is not just for keeping warm.

More men file into the room. I don't have to look closely to know it's the other splayed Fae from Aero's dungeon.

The smell of anger fills the space. They want revenge. I'd stake my life on it.

I try to swallow the bile staining my throat, my breath thickening, heart galloping along at breakneck speed.

"She smells nervous." My gaze darts to a freckle faced, red-haired man chewing on his bottom lip, worrying the bulge in his pants with the palm of a curled hand.

"Good." This one's taller than the rest, thick brows casting deep shadows across his face. His hair hangs in greasy lumps, canines on full display. He sniffs back then spits at my feet, a thick wad of saliva now clinging to my aching toes.

These men aren't just here to fuck.

They're here to kill.

I close my eyes, stomach roiling with dread.

I'm not going to make it out of here alive.

I wish there were some visible landmarks around, even a window I could catch a glimpse out of, then I could tell Aero where to find me. Even so, he's probably still sleeping … my

Sun Gods probably don't even know I'm missing, because they were out all night trying to clean up the drunken carnage I created.

Fuck.

More boots slap against the ground, someone else entering the room. "You good from here, brother?"

I recognise that fucking voice.

My *Water God* claps the Feather Plunger on the shoulder, and I gag into the material stuffed in my mouth, my body jerking as I lose control of my toes and sway like a flailing animal sliced open, hanging from a hook.

He told me I was beautiful inside and out. The fucker.

The bird eating spider clearly becomes spooked by my erratic movements, its hairy legs probing about in a fitful frenzy before its two fangs pierce the flesh on my hand, causing my entire arm to feel like it's been dipped in a furnace.

The Feather Plunger frowns and grabs a stick from the cobbled ground, pointing it above my head, using it to coax the creature down the wall. It launches itself off, landing with a gentle 'thud', front legs raised in defence, looking like it's about to charge the bastard.

I groan into my gag at the sight of it—the size of a small dinner plate with hundreds of keen, beady eyes and two fangs dripping with green liquid, that's now pulsing through my burning arm.

"Don't want that thing stinging her too much, it'll ruin all my fun," Feather Plunger drawls, using his stick to drive the creature straight out the door. It makes a nauseating squealing sound, then lands against a wall with a thump.

My head lolls to the side as my vision converges then splits, converges then splits—over and over again.

"I should leave and get back to Sterling. The Sun Gods

spent all night looking for me, I shouldn't stay in one place any longer than necessary."

Feather Plunger nods. "I'm good from here, we'll dump her down a well when we're done with her."

I groan into my gag.

My recently renamed Water Cunt nods. "Just make sure you cover your tracks. Sol looked like he actually fucking cares about this one." He prowls towards me, inspecting my body in a way you might a piece of livestock; tugging at a rope of my hair then hissing in disdain.

Fucker fooled me from the start.

The other pulls a blade from the holster around his waist, steps forward and runs the point along my chest—drawing a long, deep wound that spills ribbons of blood down my torso. I scream through the gag and he smirks, sucks air through his teeth, then runs a finger through his handiwork. The salt from his pores makes my flesh burn in protest. "Yeah, well, so did Aero." He brings his finger to his mouth and inhales the smell of my blood, eyes rolling in their sockets, then he licks the finger clean. "They're going to learn how it feels to lose something you love."

Water Cunt cocks a brow, claps his 'brother' on the shoulder and walks out. I'm left with nine leering men, shadows of their former selves, who undoubtedly blame me for the fact they lost their immortality.

Feather Plunger drags two bulging sacks into the room, followed by a chair, then a large bucket of water before closing the door behind him; latching it shut on the inside with a bolt and padlock he pulls from his pocket.

"You guys have your fun with her first," he drawls, twirling the key to the padlock between fat, dirty fingers. "I want to watch you all fuck her, but I get the rights to end the cunt." He flicks his hair from his face, looks me square in the eye and winks at me, before putting the key in his mouth and swallowing it.

Well …. fuck. It tells me enough about how long they intend to keep me in here for—until he passes that key out his arsehole, that's how long.

My head sways to the side as I fight to keep consciousness, though I'm vaguely aware of the tall man with thick brows stepping forward, pushing my thighs open and prodding at the warmth between my legs. He loosens his trousers, dropping them to his knees, and reveals a hard, spindly cock. He hauls at my body, flipping me around, causing the binds holding my wrists to tighten. My face slaps against the sodden, chilling wall when he rams his dick straight into my unsuspecting vagina.

I scream, the muffled sound reverberating about the room.

I claw at my beast lying huddled within me, begging her to do something, *anything*.

She doesn't. Instead, she coils further into a ball, cowering under the scornful gaze of the man who beat me close to death then left his mark inside my body.

My vagina's unresponsive … she now knows what it's like to be treated properly, knows where she belongs, and it's not here with these bastards.

This is the world I live in.

I'm always going to be seen as *this*—a chew toy for men to gnaw on. Nothing's going to change unless someone does something about it. Unless someone fights for the rights of the ones who no longer have a voice. But I've missed my chance. It's a devastating reality that claws at my insides, works its way up my throat, and threatens to choke me.

I squeeze my eyes shut, trying to take myself somewhere else, anywhere else … and fail. I bellow my frustrations into my gag, knowing I'm stuck here both physically *and* mentally.

I don't even have my vagina to talk to, to give me some semblance of false companionship …

I am alone.

Utterly alone.

I coil, gagging; trembling hands clutching my abdomen. There's nothing like a steel capped boot to the gut to remind you that even immortals have fragile ribs.

The noises that escape my body with the impact are far from discreet, though I see no point in keeping quiet.

Their intentions are clear.

They want me dead.

I close my eyes … breathe Dell, breathe.

I don't notice the boot careening towards my temple until it's too late.

Darkness.

A flicker of light.

My limp body being flipped over, onto my side …

Darkness.

"Are you right or left-handed, Little Pet?" The words are watery, splintered, malicious.

Coming to from the shaded haze of my semi-conscious state, I look up at my newest torturer from where I'm sprawled on the ground.

This one's new. He hasn't had a go at me yet.

His face is in shadow—eyes appearing black. Despite the harrowing darkness shading his features, the spattering of freckles across his nose and baby face make him look anything but cruel. But looks can be deceiving.

"I said …" he slaps his hand across my cheek, drawing me further from the haze. "Left, or right?"

I groan something non-committal into my gag.

"What was that?" He tugs the material out of my mouth with fingers that smell like a rotten arsehole. "I didn't quite catch it."

Cheek pressed against stone stained in piss, my hair sapping at the moisture like a thirsty sponge, I work my mouth around thin air—stretching my tongue, my jaw—trying to talk. My throat is raw, and all that comes out is a raspy groan.

"Get the bitch something to drink," the man mumbles around a cruel smirk, his canines glinting in the flickering light from the hearth. Dark shadows stretch and twist across the walls.

Most of the men are huddled around the small fire, enjoying a snack while they watch the show unfold. One of them groans, stretches, stands, and makes his way to the bucket in the corner. After scooping water into a ladle, he loiters over to us, dribbling precious liquid onto the floor in his wake.

Bastard's not even making an effort to keep the ladle steady.

My matted hair clings to my fevered face, and I curl my arms unnaturally to try and coax the pee-soaked tendrils out of my mouth, with little success.

Baby face pulls me into a kneeling position, grabbing the only chair in the room and perching it in front of me, placing my bound hands in the centre of the seat.

The message is clear.

My arse is not worthy enough to sit in the fucking chair.

The man with the ladle rounds on me, ruddy eyes shadowed and his lips thin with distaste.

I'm practically drooling over the scent of clean water.

"Thirsty?" he asks, a curious lilt tainting his voice.

I nod.

He tilts my chin so I'm looking into his pallid face. "Well then, open wide."

I do, then watch him sniff back and hurl a thick, green wad of saliva into the ladle—eyes dancing with amusement—right before he pours the contents into my mouth.

It only makes it part way down my throat before I'm throwing it back up, into my lap, all over the wooden chair that's keeping me from toppling over.

Spent, gasping for breath, mouth tainted with bile; I curl against the chair, head slung low.

Baby Face pinches my cheek, drawing my attention back to him with a flick to my ear. "Right, or left-handed, Pet?"

He has a look in his eyes that suggests withholding the answer would be a very bad idea.

"Both," I grind out, and the bastard straight up *beams*.

The one with the ladle leans against the wall, arms folded, smiling.

"Well, then …" Baby Face purrs, hauling at my bound hands and pressing them against the seat of the chair. "Sit up nice and straight now, on your knees … I want you poised and perky as you take your punishment."

He almost makes it sound nice. Like I have something to look forward to.

Slowly, I rise, manoeuvring my body into the position he instructed, against the screaming protest of my knees teetering on the cobbled floor.

"Back straight," he says, sculpting my spine, forcing me into position. "That's better." He moulds my hands, pressing them flat against the seat. I wince when he runs his finger over the bite on my right palm, making it ooze a yellow substance that smells septic …

"Ambidextrous, aye … a rare talent, that."

My heavy eyes are so busy studying the bite on my hand that I jump at the sight of the nail kissing the tip of my right index finger … and it takes longer than it usually would for me to register exactly what's about to happen.

The Feather Plunger chuckles from his spot sitting in the corner. His back's against the wall, canines gleaming while he sharpens his blade on a rock perched between his thighs. "You going to do both hands, brother?"

The hair shading his eyes makes him look utterly terrifying.

A predator.

My beast straight up quivers, despite my relentless efforts to drag the bitch out. It's like she's gone all limp dick on me.

Baby Face smirks, luring my gaze that's no longer seeking the haze of slumber, instead, wide the hell awake. He produces a hammer out of fucking nowhere, flicks it into the air, and drives the flattened head at the nail—splitting through fragile bone and sending blood splattering at my face.

I scream so loud it feels like my throat is shredding, my blood mottled arm trembling in shock, pivoting on the point where I'm now anchored to the chair.

Don't move.

Don't move.

Chest heaving, I breathe through my nose; deep, shuddering breaths, trying to control my erratic movements …

Baby Face rounds on me, running his hand up my spine and forcing me back into position. "I'll alternate, one for each hand, until she learns to keep her back straight like a good little whore."

Goddammit.

God-fucking-dammit.

He jingles a pouch, the sound of nails clinking against each other making my skin crawl. He reaches in and pulls out a long, thin one, placing the tip at the centre of my left pinkie's fingernail. "Don't forget to keep your posture in check like a good Lesser slut."

He raises the hammer.

A frightened gurgle slips past my lips.

I picture a rod strengthening my spine, keeping me still …

With a feral roar, he slams the hammer down. Another explosion of pain engulfs my body as the nail plunges through my finger and embeds deeply into the seat.

My body crumbles, back arching, stomach heaving at its meagre contents.

"Tut tut." Baby Face splays his palm across my spine. "Looks like we have to try that again."

No …

"Someone put the gag back in her mouth so I don't have to listen to the bitch whining," Feather Plunger drawls.

I shake my beast, pawing at her, *pleading* with her to wake the fuck up! To do something, *anything* to help …

Nothing.

Fucking nothing.

My bonds are snipped, and I'm thrown across the room, landing in a groaning heap of bloodied limbs and tarnished skin; my curls spewing about me in tangled disarray.

The festering wound on my hand is oozing a thick, putrid puss that's no longer yellow … it's got a slight green tinge to it now.

I slowly remove the sodden gag from my mouth with tender, trembling fingers—flicking it aside and sucking an unhindered breath.

I've been here for days … my only guide being that they all slept at least once, in front of the crackling fire, in-between sessions of filling me or beating me bloody. This time, they haven't avoided my face.

They've all had me several times, except the one who's *actually* had me before, who's been content to sit and watch my torture from his place against the wall, sharpening his blade. It's him I've been dreading the most. I know how he fucks, and he's not gentle about it.

I crack a half-swollen lid to see the object of my fractured thoughts stretch his arms dramatically, crack his back one way then the other, then pull his shirt over his head revealing a porcelain body rolling with muscle, and two gnarly scars staining his shoulder blades.

Shoulder blades which used to be the roots of his amputated wings ...

He reaches into one of the sacks, rummaging around. Many things have come out of those sacks; chains, whips, apple jam sandwiches, even a fucking tea set. They sat around and sipped a fruity, herbal blend while watching one of them repeatedly shoot his load through my hair.

I guess everyone has their kinks.

He pulls out a carrot, a branding iron, and a fucking hacksaw. I scream, a thin, wailing gurgle. I think I'm about to lose a limb or four.

He stands, pushes past a few men perched by the fire—nursing satiated grins—then stabs the branding iron into the flames, making sparks explode and embers crackle.

Fuck.

Spinning, he twirls the blade in one hand while he chews on the carrot in the other. "My turn," he spits around a mouthful of orange confetti. His eyes crinkle at the sides confirming his sick satisfaction, and he tosses the remainder of the carrot at the wall. It shatters, leaving carrot gravel scattered across the ground.

I try to scramble away, dragging my wasted body along the cobblestones, tearing at my skin as I back into a corner.

"Scared, Poppet?" He tugs on one of my legs, running the blade along the inside of my thigh, but not applying enough pressure to cut me. "You should be." He moves that blade to my clit, sneering. "Once I'm done fucking you, I'm going to carve your cunt clean off." He applies a little pressure and I temper my compulsion to gag.

Not my vagina … she's helped me so much through the years. She doesn't deserve to be scalped and *slain*.

"Then I'm going to serve it on a pretty platter for your Sun Gods to mull over, reminding them that they *aren't* that fucking powerful after all."

Tears spill, forging a path down my cheeks.

He drags me out of the corner by my ankles, my already ruined flesh catching on the uneven ground, and flips me onto my front, forcing my legs apart and tossing the blade to the side. He tugs my hips up into the air, coaxing me onto my hands and knees. "If you move," he purrs, "I'll slice your twat off while you're still alive. Got it?"

Years of conditioning has me nodding, though I can't stop the gurgled whimper from escaping my trembling lips while my beast cowers into a tight, quivering ball.

I've never seen her so frightened.

His boots thump along the ground and I hear the grind of metal against stone while he jostles the branding iron through the flames.

Snot dribbles from my nose and my tears continue to flow. My knees tremble with the effort to keep me in place, my ruined fingers throbbing … *screaming* their displeasure at being pressed against the filthy, blood smeared ground.

I know what's coming when his footsteps thump closer— my entire body trembling, muscles coiling, bracing myself for what I'm about to endure.

He presses the scalding iron to my right arsecheek. I choke—a blinding, searing pain assaulting my body, the potent scent of sizzled flesh staining my nostrils.

Limbs crumbling beneath me, I drop to the floor.

I hear the clatter of iron hitting stone.

"Stupid bitch. Now we have to try again. Up!" He boots me in the ribs. I struggle to my hands and knees, body trembling, a string of thick saliva dribbling from my heaving mouth.

"Do that again and I'll brand your face. Understand?"

I nod, focusing on the cobbled floor covered in moss, stained red with my blood. I count the cobbles in my mind—one, two, three …

He presses the iron to the same arsecheek and I breathe and count, breathe and count, concentrating on the gurgle of air fighting through snot and blood. The hiss of iron on skin is merely background noise as the reek of burning flesh thickens like a suffocating smog. I don't remember the pain being this brutal when I was last introduced to a branding iron.

When he finally pulls away, I don't have to look to know he's branded me with a giant fucking circle … just like the one that used to be present on my right palm.

A branded whore.

Only worth what pleasure my body can provide.

He tosses the branding iron to the side and pulls himself free of his pants, already rock fucking solid. He fists at it and through my bleary fog of pain, I notice the small bead of pre-cum on the tip of his cock.

This guy is one sick fuck.

"You like the look of my hard cock? It'll be the last one you ever have, you know. You'll die knowing it was *my* cock that stained the insides of that tight little pussy with my cum."

I scream, blinking away swiftly flowing tears, scrambling to get away but succeed only in curling into a quivering ball … just like my beast.

He tugs my legs open and lines himself up with my entrance.

The only way through this is to protect my mind …

I close my eyes and think of Sol, of our lovemaking still fresh in my memory …

A shiver runs up my spine.

Oh … no …

I've made a mistake …

A big.

Fucking.

Mistake.

I feel the buds of my wings begin to pierce through the muscles in my back, and I just can't stop them. They're excited to see their non-existent Day God, and I have no control over the tarts.

Perhaps I should've been practising *that* rather than collecting glowing, metallic heart tethers.

Idiot.

They're going to be so disappointed when they realise they popped out for these bastards, and not our dashing Sun God.

They unfurl—their crisp, white feathers a stark contrast to the darkness of the small room smeared with blood.

On cue, I hear a gasp and the bastard straddling me launches off, taking shuffled steps back and colliding with the others. The few who were asleep are jostled awake by the crew of slack faced sickos.

"Fuck," one of them exclaims, rubbing at his face, perspiration filming his brow.

"Not fucking possible," the Feather Plunger chokes out,

his desperate gaze darting to the brand on my arse, and back at my face.

He knows he's fucked up.

The room becomes still, the only sound that of my wings, rustling about in confusion.

Feather Plunger's watching me, eyes slits, his expression one of uncertainty. His gaze drifts to the hacksaw, cast aside, lying on the bloodied ground.

Fuck.

No.

He looks back at me with a feral sneer, his eyes glazing over, his expression one of grim determination. He stoops, picks up the hacksaw, and raises his arm … the serrated blade glinting with flickering light from the angry flame in the hearth.

No …

Not again. Not my fucking wings …

I very nearly plead with him, almost kiss his filthy boots while I beg for him to show them mercy.

They don't deserve this. They're sweet, innocent, and fragile. They're everything that's good in this world, while I'm everything that's not … darkness plagued in shadow, the stain of a society gone wrong.

We're an odd mix, but we fit perfectly together. Strangely. I can't bear to part with them again … not even in death.

My wings coil and flap in a pathetic, vain attempt at escape. They may have been four-year-old wings when they last came face to face with a hacksaw, but that probably feels like yesterday to them, and I guarantee they have the same fucked up memory I have, because they're quivering.

"Please, no … don't take my wings," I sob, scrambling, skinning my knees further, pushing him away with flailing, bloodied hands. "Anything, please, anything but them!"

He grips a wing, holding it firmly. I see the terrible glint in his eyes as he drives the saw against the sensitive skin at my wing's base. The same place Kal massages to bring me to orgasm …

It makes the bone splintering blow that much harder to swallow.

Thwack.

Thwack.

Thwack.

I let out a fractured scream and squeeze my eyes shut, pressing my face against the ground, inhaling the stench of this rotten world. I cover my ears, try to block out the terrible sound of my flapping wings as they thump against the filthy ground becoming thick and heavy with vomit, blood, and piss.

It doesn't work.

I haul myself onto my hands and knees, try to crawl away …

"Stay fucking still," he snarls, hacking at a different spot, bellowing his toxic rage as he heaves his assaults.

My limbs give way, body crumbling beneath the weight of the agony and deep sadness. Tortured feathers rain down around me.

Through the fog I register the scent of male fear, thick and musky, easily discernible from the scent of my own terror.

The bastard's terrified. Frightened of a woman splayed helpless on the ground.

Thwack.

Thwack.

Thwack.

He starts on my other wing, slashing away in a torrent of panicked frenzy. Feathers fall, blows continue to land, and my soul continues to seep from my body.

Am I dying? It's hard to kill an immortal who still has

their wings intact, but I think these fucks have almost done it.

The blows cease and I scan the floor for my discarded wings, seeing nothing but a blanket of dirty, matted feathers drenched in blood. Perhaps he's accessing a different way to finish the job, like sawing them off at the nub as my mother did.

I hear the sound of a man being tossed around, then angry, frightened voices all yelling at once … "Stay the fuck down, Drue!"

I can't move, I can barely breathe. Even my wings have given up the fight—laying limply along the back of my body, not even a tremor to tell me they're still alive back there.

"We have to kill her!" Drue bellows.

"We need to talk this through, man! Fuck!"

"What have you done? You just hacked at the fucking Princess!"

I cringe. I'm not a fucking Princess, because I refuse to be second to the man who spawned me. If they want to call me anything it better be 'Queen', or else I'm going to lose my cool and bite some cocks off. Even though I can't move, and I'm potentially dying.

I can feel blood draining from my wings, hear it dribbling onto the cold floor. I dare not take a peek. Seeing them broken, solidifying it in my mind, would probably break my heart even further.

I don't deserve wings; I'm so terrible at taking care of them.

"What do you think is going to happen, eh? That he's going to *thank* us for bringing her to him like *this*? You *know* he's been trying to breed a pure, white-winged heir!"

"A male! Not a fucking female, you idiot! He'll probably relish in the act of killing her himself like he does all the females he spawns, right before he gives us placement back in Sterling for our loyalty!"

Okay … yeah, fuck no.

Fuck no.

"Ven's right man, she could be our chance to gain back everything we lost! We can't kill her."

There's a long pause while I wait to hear their verdict.

"I think you're right … fuck."

The others grunt their approval.

"No wonder the Sun Gods liked her … she had pretty wings before you fucked them up, Drue."

Drue huffs out a laugh. It sounds cocky, though I hear the undertones …

So does my beast …

It's a laugh plagued with nervous tension that thickens my heartbeat, curls my damaged fingers, and makes the hairs on the back of my neck stand on end.

My beast flicks her ears, head emerging from the ball of fur and revealing two, sharp eyes …

He doesn't realise it yet, but I think he just became prey.

"Take a shit so we can get out of here and summon him, would ya?"

Drue grunts and I hear him shuffle around in the sack while I lay, splayed on the floor in a bloody, feathery heap; my beast prowling in circles, growling under her breath …

I mumble something incoherent, my mind scrambling for purchase as reality seems to bend around me.

"What's that, bitch?"

I have no idea what I just tried to say. I'm finding it hard to focus right now due to this shrill ringing in my ears. I can feel my sanity fraying at the seams, the essence of myself unravelling …

It seems that, finally, and at long fucking last, my beast is coming to the surface. Though, I don't expect her to come dragging this boiling cauldron of lava, the one that's so fucking hot I think it's going to burn me from the inside out.

What the actual fuck, you psycho animal? Is this like a cat bringing its owner a dead mouse?

Actually …

Lifting our head, cranking our neck to the side, we push our palms flat to the ground—ignoring the blood and feathers that are smeared about like some artistic rendition of our pain. Pain we don't feel as we push our upper body free from the ground before tugging our legs up under us.

Crouched in place, broken wings fanned behind us, the cauldron tips within—filling every part of us with painless, exquisite heat.

It doesn't frighten us.

We embrace it, sucking in a great lungful of air, and fuelling the internal blaze.

The ringing in our ears gets louder.

Slowly, we turn … keeping our eyes trained to the ground, until we know we're face to face with the group of men coagulating in the corner.

They're silent, though we sense them watching us.

Clenching our fists, we slowly raise our eyes …

The men gasp, stagger backwards, arms flailing, fumbling over each other in an effort to reach the wall.

To hide.

The ringing is almost unbearable while we take in their fearful expressions, their horrified scents. They look as if they've just glanced upon the face of death.

Perhaps they have.

We take a step forward, aware that our canines are scraping against our chin. We're also vaguely aware that our skin is glowing …

That's right. We're a naked, broken, bloody whore, and we're fucking *glowing*.

Our lips curl in approval as my beast traces my thoughts. But the heat that was a caress before is now becoming a light scald, building at our mangled fingertips, making us feel like we've dipped our hands in *very* hot water.

Our fingers twitching, we take in the scene—the men before us coated in the scent of our blood, our torture, our rape … yet reeking more predominantly of fear as they look upon *us*, a depiction of their inability to control their own beasts within.

The heat is building—we're surprised our hands aren't on fire. We take a peek down, just to make sure, gulping at the lump in our throat.

A cold smile curls at the edges of our lips. We slowly raise our left palm, purposefully shifting our gaze to one of the bastards before us … the one who did terrible things to us with that cattle prod over there.

The one who has piss running down his legs.

We squeeze our palm shut, and he fucking *explodes*.

Poof, just like that.

A spray of red mist coats the room as his body disintegrates into nothing more than a cloud of blood—the scald on our hand subsiding to a dull warmth.

The remaining men fumble around, horror staining their features.

I want to vomit, even though my beast wants to roll around in the filth and fucking bathe in it.

The men are screaming, huddling together, jostling to be at the back. But our right hand is burning, so we choose our next target … Baby Face. The man who put a nail through most of our fingertips.

We raise our palm, pointing it in his direction.

He scrambles away, cowers in the corner, shits himself.

Unlike my beast, I feel a slight pang of remorse, right before we pump our fist and make the fucker go *poof*.

We're coated in blood. Mine, theirs, and the blood of every woman who has ever suffered in this cruel, dark world.

Drue is trying to hide behind the rest of them, but we're not going to turn him into crimson mist … no, no. We have another plan for him entirely. My beast has planned it explicitly, and she's fucking salivating over the idea.

The ringing in our ears is low now, low enough for us to clearly hear their pleads for mercy. It almost works.

Our vision starts to flicker, my beast battling to stay present.

We're running on fumes.

I look to the cauldron within us, still full to the rim. It's our *body* that's started to give out.

Fuck.

We point through the crowd, directly at Drue. "Give us him," we rasp, our voice a crumbled melody of darkness.

The men oblige, grabbing at the Feather Plunger and throwing him forward, despite his dramatic pleads for mercy. He fumbles across the ground, losing his footing and landing at our feet, crying at us for clemency.

Funny—watching a man fall at the feet of a woman—seeing the fear in his eyes as he begs time and time again for us to spare his life … to spare his fucking *soul*.

If I were in control, I'd possibly fold …

But I'm not, and he's not pleading to a saint … he's pleading to my beast, and she has no interest in showing this fucker an ounce more mercy than he showed us.

We pluck the hacksaw from his white knuckled hand, scenting the urine pooling beneath him.

We're surprised when he doesn't fight—he doesn't even try to stop what he must realise is inevitable. Perhaps he can see it on our face, the conviction in our movements … we're not fucking around.

Or perhaps he thinks that what we have planned is a

lesser punishment than going *poof.*

If that is the case, he couldn't be more wrong.

We kneel next to him, running our finger over his bare chest, drawing swirls mindlessly in the blood staining his skin. I'm shocked when I see the giant rendition of a cock on his flesh. Guess my beast is trying to say she's about to fuck him with her beast schlong.

We place the hacksaw against the smooth, sensitive skin of his belly, holding it there while the terrible reality of what we are about to do dawns on him. His eyes widen and he opens his mouth to plead, but instead his scream pierces the fetid air when we slice into his flesh, dragging the serrated blade through skin, muscle, and hard, sinewy tendons. He tries to fight, but his efforts are futile, his pathetic clawing weakening while blood pours out of him in scarlet ribbons.

Smiling, we pull his intestines free, threading them through our fingers and pulping them delicately, as if preparing a meal.

We push along something hard, feel for its edges, confirming it's the correct shape. Never know, he could have a bizarre affliction for swallowing strange shit.

We smile. It's definitely the key.

A small part of my mind is aware of just how fucked up this scene must look, the part that's drowning in the sea of rage and self-preservation.

We point to one of the fear-stricken men, one of the minorities who hasn't passed out from the sight of all this gore. "Come here."

He does, like an obedient dog, bowing before us.

We slice the hacksaw straight through the Feather Plunger's colon, who immediately passes the fuck out. To be fair, we're surprised he lasted so long.

"Put your hand out."

The man does so, his palm painted with sweat and blood.

We pop the shit smeared key into his hand.

"Go wash it off," we order, standing, wiping our hands on our bare skin and remembering we're butt naked, aside from all the blood. "And give us your fucking shirt."

He peels it off faster than we've ever seen a whore lose her clothes, tossing the shirt to us before moving to the corner and rinsing the key in a bowl on the ground, the one the men have been using to wash their hands. It's probably more cum than water at this point.

We undo a few of the shirt buttons at the top to accommodate what's left of our wings, then bend down and step into it backwards, putting our arms through the holes and tugging it over our shoulders. It falls to about mid-thigh, our lack in height bringing some advantage by allowing the man's top to cover our exposed twat.

The shirt smells like the bastard, but it's better than walking out that door butt naked. Who knows where the hell we might be right now? Probably in the middle of a town square somewhere—if we walk out naked, we'll draw some undue attention and my beast will be forced to make some more bastards go *poof*.

With the clean key in our hand, we signal for the man to join the rest of the group, which he does without hesitation, reeking of fear, piss, and shit ... predominantly his own.

We've never made a man shit himself before, and we've just managed three in the space of a few short minutes, if you count the one we sliced open.

In our defence, he *did* threaten to cut off our vagina. *Nobody* threatens our fucking vagina.

A wave of lethargy hits, vertigo tugging at our ability to stand up straight as the warmth coating our insides begins to drain away, along with the remaining droplets of our strength.

We walk to the door. Trying to look like a badass even

though we're fairly certain we're about to pass out, we use the key to jiggle the bolt open with trembling hands, then swing the door wide.

The remaining men stand huddled in a growing pool of piss. "Follow us, and we'll paint the walls with your blood." Our voice echoes off the walls, full of shaded malice and bearing little resemblance to my own. We sashay out into a dark hallway, with only the distant scent of fresh air wafting through to guide us.

We turn and follow our nose for a good few minutes before it occurs to us that we should have locked the bastards in there. We're not going back though, not after that final speech about painting the walls with their blood. It would ruin an epic fucking epilogue …

Dragging our throbbing hand along the cobbled wall that's dripping in fuck knows what—hoping like hell we don't run into another one of those Fae biting spiders—we stumble on uneven ground and fall face first into the steps rising before us.

Boasting a few more bruises, cuts, and probably even a broken nose, we crawl up the steps, slowly dragging our broken body away from the stench of fear and death.

Panting, muscles trembling, dribbling sweat despite the chill, we emerge into a blanket of pitch black, gulping back fresh lobs of air, our hands and legs dragging through freshly tilled soil draped with dead leaves and twigs.

Caped in darkness, we haul ourselves into a standing position, waver, and put one unsteady foot in front of the other, trying not to trip and fall on the shrubs littering the ground.

My beast coils around herself *and* that fucking cauldron, then disappears altogether.

Bitch.

Alone again, I stumble through the darkness, bleary-eyed,

bloody, and broken. The watery light from a wavering moon breaks through the clouds and I see it too late—a jutting rock. I hit it with my calf, tumble over and catapult into a river of icy cold water.

That wakes me up.

It feels like a dream, a plagued nightmare as I'm sucked into the rushing turmoil, swept over rocks, dragged against sticks and debris, not even *fighting* for breath …

It occurs to me that I lost a part of myself tonight. Perhaps even something integral. I lost a part of my soul, and I fucking *revelled* in it …

Who am I?

Who am I becoming?

Now, more than ever, I hate myself. Because now? I'm just as bad as *them*. I'm just as bad as the fuckers who've destroyed me time and time again—the same men who've condemned this world to rot.

I'm my father's daughter. Am I predestined to follow in his footsteps, leaving a bloody stain on a world already ruined? Am I just as bad as … *him*?

I'm probably drowning, and I hate that my last act on this world was to blow two fuckers up and gut another. If I could take it back, I would.

I may be dying, but the implications of that are muted. Because above all? I feel sick.

Sick with guilt.

Sick with … *remorse*.

Fuck.

As I'm pushed down a collaboration of rolling rapids that are less than kind to my already broken body, I realise I'm not like them at all—all those men who've left such a blemish on this world, *because* I have remorse. Because I recognise the monster within myself, aware that I'm equal parts dark and light … and I did what I had to do to *survive*.

I don't have to be a saint to make an impact on the world … I just have to be me.

Because I'm enough.

I've always been enough.

Who am I?

I'm the child who witnessed her father kill her mother. The girl who fell in love with the man who sold her body for a living.

I'm a branded whore, I even enjoyed it at times.

I'm a woman who's been broken time and time again, moulded into an object of male desire, and forced to comply in a society that's poisoned with obscurity.

There's not much left of my sanity, but I survived. I'm *more* than who I was born to be, because I'm a *survivor*.

I become aware of a sharp burning sensation in my lungs, a cool darkness threatening to overwhelm me while the rapids toss me about like a giant, watery hand hauling me this way and that.

I'm a *survivor*.

I kick, trying to find leverage in the stony, crumbling ground rushing beneath me. My feet give way and I flounder, arms flailing … drifting, drifting, bubbles cascading around me.

My legs drag against something hard and jagged, the sting of torn flesh like fire against the icy chill of the raging current. My feet find traction and I push upwards, finally breaking the surface, dragging a deep bout of bitter air into my lungs …

I refuse to give up.

I will fucking *live.*

Who am I?

I'm the damaged heir to a broken empire.

My name is Adeline Sterling, and it's time my father learnt the true value of a woman's worth.

CHAPTER FOURTEEN

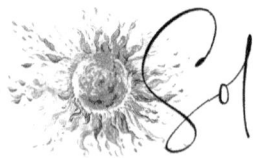

The sun caresses my face, rousing me out of the
deepest fucking sleep of my very long life. My
mind is heavy, stretched … emotionally hungover. I don't
do 'emotions' very well, never have. I prefer to keep that
shit locked up, rather than evoke a weakness in my
shield.

I've never had a reason to drop the walls before. Never
wanted one.

Until now.

In the end, handing that intimate part of myself to Dell
was the easiest fucking thing I've ever done.

I look inside myself to where I'm cradling that sterling
tether attached to my heart like a fucking pussy, wondering
how the hell I ever coped without it. My little mate fits me so
perfectly … like a glove specifically created for both my soul
and my cock.

Groaning, still half asleep, I rub my palm against my
pulsing rod, hard and ready for her again. It's like she's put a
spell on my dick. I swear to fuck, if she asked him to jump,
he'd bounce up and down saying 'how high?' I'd probably be

pissed off about the lack of self-control if I didn't enjoy it so much.

If Drake thinks he's going to be the first to plant his seed inside her, he's got another thing coming.

Fuck.

I barely recognise this version of myself.

The moment her soul kissed mine, I knew I was screwed. Fucking *done.* I realised I'd not only met my match, but something far, far more.

Dell is the answer to the riddle this world keeps choking on, because it chewed her up and somehow still spat her out whole. The others think it was her heritage which gave her body the fortitude to survive those years in the darkness— the shit she had to endure.

I disagree. It's much simpler than that.

She's been through the fucking worst this world has to offer, and for most of the time, I was none the wiser as it tore away at pieces of my mate. Some might say she lost herself through it all … I say she's fucking incredible. While pieces of her crumbled, my glorious little Queen protected the most important bits, fortifying them over time, moulding herself into something formidable … whether she realised it or not.

She's everything this fucked up world needs. More. She's everything I fucking need.

She's a beacon of hope. The brightest fucking light. How did I miss her all these years? It's something I'll never forgive myself for. I'll always hold myself partially responsible for the shit she's been through, and I intend to spend the rest of eternity making it up to her.

She's mine now. I'd go to Death's fucking doorway so that woman could continue to breathe.

She doesn't understand the implications of what her and I just did together, what she willingly *gave* to me … but she fucking will.

Opening my eyes, I lift my hand to shield my face from the glare as my morning Dell-induced wood becomes too stiff to bear any longer. If she's still asleep, she's about to wake to my cock sliding between those pretty white thighs. I twitch at the thought.

"Do you remember your safe word?"

No answer.

I roll over, see she's gone. Frowning, I draw a deep whiff of air.

Something smells … off.

"Dell?"

Silence.

She's probably bathing. She did run her mouth earlier about my seed crusting down her thighs, right before I tied her wrists to her ankles and licked, nipped, and fucked her all over while she squealed my name so loud that I had to compel Aero to fucking walk back to his room. Nosey bastard. Like fuck was I going to share Dell with him on our mating night.

I climb out of bed and walk to the door of the bathing chamber, expecting to see my glorious, white-winged goddess lounging in the water, soaking herself clean of my seed.

It's empty.

That white tether on my heart fucking *tugs*, becoming so taut my hand flies to my chest in an effort to soothe the strain.

Fuck.

Is she regretting our bond? *Fighting* it? If she tears it out it'll fucking *kill her*.

"*Dell?*"

I grab my discarded pants, dragging them on, my cock pointing at the sky when Drake steps out of the Bright and straight into my fucking bedroom.

His nostrils flare, eyes wide, wings fanning out, his dark side permeating me with a poisonous glare. He pulls his lips back from his teeth and fucking *hisses* at me.

I flick my wings out wider, puff out my chest, and bare my canines at the fuckwit, filling as much space as I can. "Put them away!" I roar, because I don't have time for this shit.

I should have known it was too good to be true. Should have known she would fucking *regret* it.

"*What have you done to her?*" Drake growls, hand clutching at his chest, clawing at his flesh like he's trying to hold it together … just like me.

Fuck …

I try to keep my voice calm as I answer, though I don't *feel* fucking calm. "I mated with her, then we slept. You hurting?"

He's suddenly in my face, nose to nose, the scent of his desire to rip my throat out potent and desperate. "Yes," he grinds, and I can sense his vulnerability, the pain he's feeling that isn't his own … because he's my brother in all sense other than blood. I know the fucker like I know my left hand.

He's not in pain. He's in fucking *agony*. *Her* agony.

"Drake …" I say, watching his beast lose the battle.

I'm slammed with the full brunt of his power, like ten thousand nails hammering into my organs.

Motherfucker.

I grit my teeth, body filling with warmth before I swiftly expel it, sending my will to take hold of his limbs and secure him in place, though it doesn't stop the continual flow of 'fuck you cunt' he's sending straight to my insides.

Dell thinks I'm the overpowered one. She's wrong. There's a reason Drake has so much control most of the time. Because if he loses it? *This* happens. The pain I'm experiencing right now, it's enough to kill a regular mortal. Fuck, it's enough to kill an immortal High Fae. The only reason I'm not falling from the blow is because I'm drawn from the same fucking cast as this brutal bastard.

Beads of sweat are trailing both our faces as I try and gather the grit to talk. I gasp a few breaths, making an odd sort of groaning sound and his eyeballs narrow, the white in them entirely suffocated.

He's deep. He's really fucking deep ...

"Stop ... Dell ... *danger...*"

The agony thickens as his beast dishes me an extra layer of malice and I fall to my knees, barely registering the pain of them crashing against the floor with Drake making me feel like he's tearing me limb from fucking limb.

Kal and Aero blast their way out of the Bright, just when I think I'm about to pass the fuck out.

Drake falls to sleep, thudding to the ground in a golden heap of muscle. I curl forward in a heaving mess, thanking the Sun for the neutralising bastard that's Kal, even if he does have better abdominal muscles than me.

Aero's clutching at his head like it's caught in a vice, his skin a tepid grey as he grits his teeth against something only he can hear.

"The fuck happened?" Kal seethes, checking Drake's pulse. He probably had to dish him an extra layer just to get the bastard to respond. He gives more than us, trying to keep the peace since everything went to shit. I can tell it's starting to take its toll. "I had to triple dose him! Fuck ..." He slaps Drake on the side of his face, hard, probably making sure the cunt's still breathing.

I couldn't give a fuck about Drake right now though, he'll live. That sterling tether is tearing at my chest, I'm not sure I'm as confident about the fate of my mate.

"She's not okay," Aero groans, visibly wrangling his dark side for purchase. "She's not fucking okay!"

"Tell me everything!" I roar, working to uncurl my body, turning to face Aero.

He looks heavy, weighed down. His gift takes its toll, too.

He can't escape it. Ever.

Aero shakes his head, levelling me with a glare that tells me everything I need to know.

"Who *the fuck* has her?" That tether tugs again, my hand flying to my chest. Hand on his own chest, Drake writhes on the ground in his sleep.

When Aero doesn't answer, I spear my glare at Kal, hair dishevelled, and black sleeping pants slung low on his hips.

"Don't look at me! He woke me up by dragging me through the Bright with him! I'm just as much in the fucking dark as you are!"

Aero claws at his hair, face sharpening as he wrestles his beast. He's going to have to wrestle mine too if he doesn't hurry the fuck up, because the brutal fuck is tearing at me from the inside, desperate to break free and hunt our mate down himself. He chose her just as much as I did … if we lose her? Something tells me that a part of me won't survive it.

Aero paces, shaking his head. He drops down, kneeling on the ground, cradling his head in his hands.

Kal and I share a look, converging towards him.

The silence, the anticipation, is destroying me from the inside out. Not for the first time since we met Dell, I wish I had his fucking gift. "*Aero … fucking answer me!*"

"I'm trying to concentrate!" he roars, refusing to meet my gaze, lost in his own head. Lost in hers …

I pace the room, give my body something to do other than stand there looking like a fool. I'm not good at this, standing around … waiting.

"There's more than one," he finally grinds out, halting me in my tracks.

Kal's hiss shreds through the space between us. "What the fuck's that supposed to mean?" He levels me with a lethal stare. "How the fuck did you lose track of her?"

I don't know how to answer. She was right here ...

If something happens to her, there's only me to blame.

Aero screams into his hands, snatching our attention, sending his anger out in a palpable wave; his features sharpening as his wings unfurl from his body.

Kal shoots me a look, all animosity between us disintegrating as we recognise the greater threat right now.

Aero's untameable beast.

I know what he's asking with that one look alone. One nod and he'll put the savage bastard to sleep, too. But I won't do it. We need him. We need as much information as we can get ... or something tells me we won't see her again.

I won't accept that. I'll never fucking accept that.

I stride forward, coming to stand before Aero.

He crouches, hissing into his hands, slowly losing himself to the only connection we have with Dell.

"Focus, brother. Fucking *focus*. She needs us." I don't know how I sound so calm. I'm not calm. I've got a fucking storm raging inside me.

Aero stands, muscles coiled, canines lengthening as his eyes become shadowed pools.

"Hold it in, Dawn. Hold it fucking in!" I grasp his shoulders and he roars, glaring at me with a feral gaze.

Kal shifts beside me, his voice firm and calm, no doubt dishing Aero tendrils of the happy stuff to gently level him out again, though hopefully not enough that he loses himself entirely. "We need *you*, Aero! Dell fucking needs you! Come back, brother ..."

Aero's eyes lighten, his canines retreat, and he looks at us, trembling, visibly exhausted. He slowly shakes his head, sweat beading at his brow.

"What? What is it?" My own beast is sniffing the air, ready to pounce …

He drops to a crouching position, shoulders slumped, shadowed face drawn. "That's all I'm getting. She's filtering her *fucking* thoughts again."

"Not the king?" Kal asks.

Silence fills the space for seconds, minutes, while Aero continues to listen. "No," he finally says, with an exhale of breath. "Not the King."

"Thank fuck," I hiss.

Aero stills, listening again, gaze distant, head cocked to the side.

I know something's coming, can feel it in the air. Can feel it flooding from my brother before me.

He pulls in a shuddering breath, scent thickening, closing his eyes and clenching his fists.

Fear.

He's fucking *afraid*.

Aero says the words that chill me to the bone. "They won't let her leave alive."

My beast roars beneath my skin, tearing through my confines and breaking his way to the surface. "Are you fucking sure?" we growl, deep and guttural, in a voice that doesn't sound like my own … because it's not.

It belongs to both of us.

Aero matches our gaze with his own, has the good mind not to flinch as he looks upon the face of my inner darkness.

I can feel myself dripping the malice my beast wants to inflict on the fuckers who sought to harm our mate. He's salivating for their blood. We both are.

Aero nods. Once. Slowly … "Positive. And I have no idea where they are. Neither does she."

My beast tears into the Bright without another thought.

We'll find her.

We'll tear the world to fucking shreds if we have to.
We *will* find her ...

The end of book three.

ACKNOWLEDGMENTS

Thank you, Mum and Dad. You are a pillar of support and have always urged me to follow my dreams. I never expected those dreams would compel me to write a story about a prostitute who has conversations with her vagina, but we'll ignore that finer detail. I know you are proud of me, and that's all that matters!

Mum, when I read you the first chapter of book one of this series, you never once batted an eyelid at all the slippery vaginas, never once told me I should write something more pertinent. In fact, you proceeded to sit down and brainstorm the rest of the series with me while we laughed hysterically over highly inappropriate innuendo.

Thank you for making me feel validated every day of my life. Thank you for the countless hours you have spent helping me to polish my work. I couldn't have done this without you.

My darling husband - thank you for believing in me, for reminding me of my untapped potential ... I bet you never expected it would spurt onto the pages of a book in the form of a reverse harem, huh?! (Insert laughing face here) But in all seriousness, thank you for sticking it out with me.

Nana, thank you for inspiring me with your creativity, and for showing me how strong and independent a woman can be. I love you, and not a day goes by that I don't miss you.

Lauren, thank you for the hours you invest into helping me. I can't wait to repay the favour when you release your first book. Most importantly, thank you for laughing at my vulgar sense of humour and dishing it right back at me.

Chinah, thank you for all your amazing suggestions, and I'm forever awed by your incredible copy editing skills! Not to mention all the brainstorming sessions, pushing me to take my writing to the next level.

Brittani, thank you for all the hours you pour into proofing for me, for being so thorough, and for constantly bringing sunshine and laughter to our little BETA team!

Angelique, thank you for your ongoing support. For loving these characters and making me feel such incredible validation!

Talarah, I couldn't be without your endless support and encouragement. Thank you for being you, and for always bringing a smile to my face!

To everyone else who has supported me along this journey that has only just begun, thank you!

ABOUT THE AUTHOR
SARAH ASHLEIGH PARKER

Sarah is New Zealand born and lives in the Gold Coast, Australia with her husband and their three children. She discovered her love for the written word early on, devouring book after book and creating her own stories in her spare time, winning various competitions throughout her school years for her quirky imagination.

It's only recently that she has been able to fully immerse herself into writing, being at home with three young children and an unquenchable thirst for creativity.

And so, with the timing being as good as it ever gets, and the passion and determination of a woman possessed, Sarah threw herself into becoming an author. Juggling an eclectic mix of manic writing, editing and proofing sessions, child rearing, homemaking and everything else life throws around, she somehow makes it work.

Sarah's preferred genre is adult fantasy romance and contemporary romance.

Printed in Great Britain
by Amazon